# WAR UNDER THE PACIFIC

The U.S. Navy had to know why a dozen I-class Japanese submarines had secretly gathered in Tokyo Bay. Fleet Submarine *Shark* was dispatched to discover what the enemy was planning. Through dangerous enemy waters thick with destroyers and patrols, through mine fields and an impregnable steel harbor net, the men of the *Shark* attempted one of the most daring reconnaissance missions of the war, straight into the heart of the Japanese fleet.

# "Courage Runs Deep"

# THE SUBMARINERS:
# MISSION TOKYO BAY

BY
CLAY AND JOAN BLAIR

BANTAM BOOKS
TORONTO · NEW YORK · LONDON

THE SUBMARINERS: MISSION TOKYO BAY
*A Bantam Book / January 1980*

*The U.S. Navy Submarine Service insignia courtesy
of Submarine Force Library & Museum,
Naval Submarine Base, Groton, Connecticut.*

*All rights reserved.
Copyright © 1979 by Clay and Joan Blair.
Cover art copyright © 1979 by Bantam Books, Inc.
This book may not be reproduced in whole or in part, by
mimeograph or any other means, without permission.
For information address: Bantam Books, Inc.*

ISBN 0–553–13412–4

*Published simultaneously in the United States and Canada*

*Bantam Books are published by Bantam Books, Inc. Its trade-
mark, consisting of the words "Bantam Books" and the por-
trayal of a bantam, is Registered in U.S. Patent and Trademark
Office and in other countries. Marca Registrada. Bantam
Books, Inc., 666 Fifth Avenue, New York, New York 10019.*

PRINTED IN THE UNITED STATES OF AMERICA

# CHAPTER ONE

The fleet submarine *Shark* wallowed heavily in an oily following sea. It was a moonless night with no breeze. The six men on bridge watch searched the dark horizon more intently than usual. *Shark* lay astride the Japanese convoy routes from the Marianas to Japan—a busy spot in the northern reaches of the Bonin Islands—and the SJ surface-search radar was temporarily out of commission.

At 0134, Willie Bonsel, one of three lookouts who were standing on a platform in the periscope shears, broke the silence on the bridge. "Smoke on the horizon. Zero-three-zero."

The contact had apparently not fazed Fireman Bonsel, who was noted for his taciturnity, but the other five men on the bridge were electrified. Especially the quartermaster, Jack Childress, fresh out of sub school and making his first war patrol. When he swung his 7-by-50 binoculars to the horizon off the starboard bow, his hands trembled so badly he could not focus the lens.

The officer of the deck, Jim Bell, a reserve lieutenant, junior grade, who was *Shark's* communications officer, riveted his binoculars on the horizon and spoke quietly but authoritatively into the intercom to the conning tower immediately below: "Report to the captain. Smoke on the horizon. Zero-three-zero. Come right to two-five-oh. Secure the battery charge. Put all four main engines on the line. All ahead full."

*Shark* suddenly came awake, a lethal predator

1

on the scent of prey. Belowdecks, the word spread quickly. Men on watch laid aside coffee cups and knocked off idle chatter. Topside, Jim Bell heard the throaty rumble of the diesel engines speeding up and saw the wake outline a sharp turn to starboard. Bell was a civilian-sailor, a civil engineer by trade, a bit stodgy, with a tendency to take himself too seriously, but in three patrols on *Shark* he had learned his duties well. He spoke again into the intercom: "Radar. How much longer will you be out of commission?"

A voice responded, "Another two—three minutes." It was Al Weir. In the ship's organization, Weir, the sole radar technician, came under Bell's jurisdiction, along with the radiomen and sonarmen. Weir was very bright, but a difficult personality in the confined atmosphere of a submarine. Arrogant. Legalistic. Never said "sir" to an officer. A pain in the ass most of the time, yet indispensable, for they all depended on the SJ radar—for search, for attack, and for navigation in confined waters.

Jim Bell could sense the captain coming up the hatch. He kept his binoculars riveted on the smoke wisps and edged over to make room.

Jack Mills, the captain, a brawny man of thirty-two, had immense shoulders and a size-twenty neck. At the Naval Academy, when he was voted all-American tackle, the sportswriters had aptly tagged him Mauler Mills. Football had always been his first love. In high school, he'd been all-city quarterback, then all-state; and after the Academy, while putting in his obligatory two years' big-ship duty on the *California*, he'd coached a Pacific Fleet team through two undefeated seasons. He received many offers to play pro ball, and he was just about to resign his commission and join the Detroit Lions when the Japanese attacked Pearl Harbor.

Mills's huge frame was clad in rumpled khakis, and he sported a red baseball cap. Though only minutes out of a dead sleep, his clear blue eyes were alert and all seeing. And, as always, his first thoughts were of his men.

"Who spotted it, Jim?" Mills asked Bell, raising his binoculars.

"Willie the Silent."

Mills turned and shouted up to Bonsel, "What kind of booze do you drink, Willie?"

"Scotch, sir," Bonsel called down, vastly pleased with himself. When they reached port, he would receive a quart of scotch, the Old Man's standing reward for sighting a Japanese contact without help from radar. No small deal. A quart of scotch in Pearl Harbor—if it could be found at all—sold for fifty dollars on the black market. Even counting the fifty percent pay bonus for submarine duty, that was better than two weeks' pay for Bonsel.

Al Weir spoke on the intercom. "Radar back on the line. Contact bearing two-five-oh. Range one-two-oh-oh-oh. It looks like a convoy."

Mills replied quietly to the intercom, "Very well. Station the tracking party."

The tracking party consisted of four men whose leader was Shark's number two, or executive officer, Mike Reynolds. Using continuous ranges and bearings from radar, as well as ingenuity, these men would hand-plot the course and speed of the enemy convoy, fundamental data for planning an attack. Within a few minutes they had manned their station—a plotting table in the control room—and presently, Mike Reynolds reported to Mills on the intercom. "Captain. Enemy course oh-one-two. Speed eleven. Nominal zigzag plan Baker."

"Very well," Mills replied. "Good work, Mike."

Al Weir came on the intercom next. "Captain, I count fourteen pips now. Ten big ships in two columns of fives. Four escorts: ahead, astern, and on both flanks. Range one-oh-oh-oh-oh."

Jack Mills had not been an outstanding scholar

at the Academy. He was middle of the class, mediocre in English, but he was blessed with an uncanny ability to visualize an enemy formation. Someone at the attack trainer in the sub school in New London had called it spatial vision. When Mills discovered his talent, he attributed it to football discipline: long years of sizing up a defensive formation on the gridiron and the instantaneous changes that ensued after the ball was snapped. Now, digesting the flow of data from all sources, Mills routinely and automatically visualized a plan of attack. But he held it to himself. Tonight he had a surprise up his sleeve. An innovation.

"Go to battle stations," he said quietly into the intercom.

A soft gong rang seventeen times throughout the boat. All eighty-six men on Shark hurried to their battle stations, and within one minute, Mike Reynolds, now in the conning tower, reported, "All hands at battle stations, Captain." During an attack, Reynolds was the assistant approach officer, second-in-command assisting the captain. On a night surface attack, Mills remained on the bridge, Reynolds in the conning tower, supervising the attack party.

Mills said, "Mike, can you come up here?"

"Aye, sir," Reynolds replied in a puzzled tone.

Reynolds made his way up the ladder to the bridge. He was pale faced now, a tall man but slight, and concave chested. Two years behind Mills in age and Naval Academy class, he had made seven consecutive war patrols on Shark, climbing the wardroom ladder from communications officer to first lieutenant to engineering officer to exec, and he was now fully qualified to command Shark.

Mills unfolded his surprise. "Mike, I want you to take the boat and make the attack. I'll go below and be your assistant approach officer."

Reynolds choked down a cry of delight. "Aye, aye, sir," he managed. He was stunned and proud all at once. Had he had any chest at all, it would have swelled. It was Mills's unorthodox way of expressing confidence—and of putting him to the ultimate test. If he did well, he knew Mills would recommend him for his own command, even though he was only class of 1937. A recommendation from Jack Mills would carry immense weight at headquarters.

Easing down the hatch to the conning tower, Mills had some last words for his protégé. "Good luck, Mike. Good hunting."

# CHAPTER TWO

The conning tower was dimmed out and jammed with battle-station personnel. Al Weir on radar; Roger Jones, the pharmacist's mate, on sonar; Seaman Frank Nalle on the helm; another seaman on the sound-powered telephone. Jim Bell and Wally Yates, the engineering officer, manned the most sophisticated piece of fire-control gear on the boat, the torpedo data computer, or TDC. Mounted vertically on the bulkhead, it looked like a pinball machine that presented the attack plan with lights, lines, and arrows and automatically set the gyro steering mechanisms in the torpedoes to hit the enemy targets.

Mills pushed his way aft to the TDC and laid a friendly hand on Jim Bell's shoulder. Bell and Yates were seated on stools in front of the TDC, putting in data with little cranks. "Mike's going to make the attack," Mills said. "I'm the assistant approach officer. We'll give him all the help he needs, but it's his ball game. He's calling his own plays."

Word of this unorthodox procedure spread through the conning tower, and the telephone talkers passed it on to the other ten compartments below. "Mr. Reynolds is making the attack." Everyone knew why: the Old Man was giving Reynolds his graduation test.

Reactions varied. Those who had felt Reynolds's lash at captain's mast—the exec was a son of a bitch on discipline—prayed he would do well and move on to a boat of his own. But many were uneasy that the boat had been placed in different hands.

"Range six-oh-oh-oh," Weir reported. They were closing on the enemy formation. Three miles to go.

"Very well," Reynolds replied. His voice had a ring of confidence as he went on setting up the attack. "We'll shoot all ten tubes. Three at the big freighter—the second ship in the far column. Three at the tanker leading the near column. And two each at the second and third ships in the near column. Depth set, six feet."

"Aye, aye, sir," Jim Bell responded, repeating the target selections and firing sequence.

Mills nodded silently, but he was a trifle disappointed. Reynolds's attack plan was the standard textbook solution. Mills reminded himself that it was Reynolds's ball game. Reynolds was orthodox, textbook oriented. The solution was to be expected.

On the bridge, Reynolds turned to the battle-station quartermaster, Chief Petty Officer Bob Pierpont. "Keep a sharp eye on that port flanker escort. Let me know everything he does."

"Aye, aye," Pierpont replied.

There was little love lost between these two. The Old Man had brought Pierpont with him from *Trout*. Pierpont had been a star running back on Mills's fleet team before the war, and thus he enjoyed a special status on *Shark*. This offended Reynolds, whose view of enlisted men had been shaped by years of growing up on navy bases, the son of a Naval Academy graduate and a Washington socialite.

Pierpont regarded Reynolds as a typical navy brat, a spoiled snob. He understood that Mills required a shit for an exec because Mills himself was too soft on discipline, but he thought Reynolds carried his role too far.

"All ahead two-thirds, open the outer doors," Reynolds commanded. He was hunched over the target bearing transmitter, or TBT: a pair of binoculars mounted over a dimly lighted gyro compass repeater. He sighted the binocular cross hairs on his first target, pushed a buzzer, and the bearing was automatically relayed to the TDC.

They were very close now. Pierpont, his binoculars riveted on the starboard escort—a fleet destroyer—could *smell* the Japanese ships.

"Final bearing!" Reynolds sang out, his eyes still glued to the TBT. *"Mark!"*

At the TDC, Bell replied quietly, "Distance to the track, one-one-oh-oh. Solution light."

"Very well," Reynolds replied, equally calmly. "Stand by to shoot." Three seconds passed. "Fire one! Fire two! Fire three!"

Three torpedoes swooshed from the forward tubes.

"All tubes fired electrically," reported Bell.

"Very well," said Reynolds, looking at the three torpedo wakes. "Running hot, straight, and normal. Stand by for the second target." He returned his eyes to the TBT, fixing the cross hairs on the tanker leading the near column. "Final bearing. *Mark!*"

"Solution!"

"Fire four! Fire five! Fire six!"

"All tubes fired electrically."

"Right full rudder," Reynolds commanded, swinging the boat to bring the stern tubes to bear. He fixed the TBT cross hairs on the second ship in the near column. Another freighter.

In the conning tower, Mills stood behind Bell and Yates, watching for error. Two good men, he thought, cool as cucumbers. So far, so good.

"Final bearing," Reynolds called on the TBT. "*Mark!*"

Pierpoint, binoculars on the escort, listened with grudging admiration. Reynolds was a shit, but he knew his job. This was going to be one sweet attack.

At that instant, there was a cataclysmic explosion in the convoy. The first three torpedoes had hit the big freighter in the far column, and the ship blew with awesome force. None of them had ever seen anything like it. Flames surged up to five hundred feet, lighting the sea brightly, and a searing shock wave blasted *Shark*'s bridge.

"Keeeerist!" Pierpont cried.

Reynolds was cool. "Looks like an ammo ship, captain," he said. "Fire seven! Fire eight!"

"We can feel the heat down here," Mills said. "Good shooting."

Five seconds later the second salvo of torpedoes slammed into the lead tanker in the near column. The explosion was not so spectacular, but the ship burst into flames. "Tanker hit and burning," Reynolds shouted at the intercom.

Pierpont kept his binoculars on the starboard escort. He could see every detail plain as day. Men were running all over her deck to battle stations, and her green yardarm signal lights were blinking frantically. A sailor on the bridge lifted a Very pistol and fired a red flare over the convoy as a cloud of soot belched from her single raked stack. She was putting on steam.

"Check fire!" Reynolds sang out. His fourth target had abruptly veered out of formation, and the whole convoy was now thrashing into confusion. Reynolds swung the TBT to a smaller transport. "New setup. Stand by. *Mark!*"

Pierpont saw the destroyer turn. "Starboard escort turning toward," he reported coolly to Reynolds. "Angle on the bow zero." The words were scarcely out of his mouth when he saw the destroyer's forward turret enveloped in flame —it was a muzzle blast. "Incoming mail!" he shouted.

The 4.5-inch shell wooshed over *Shark*, smashing the water a hundred yards ahead. Close. Much too close.

"Check fire!" Reynolds shouted. "Right full rudder. All ahead emergency." He would chase the splashes, standard evasion procedure to confuse the Japanese gunners. But for how long, Pierpont wondered. The destroyer would overtake them quickly. When would Reynolds dive the boat?

Another shell fell close off the port bow. "Left full rudder!" Reynolds cried into the intercom. Then he turned, cupped his hands, and shouted, "Lookouts! Clear the bridge!"

The three lookouts swung out of the shears, dropped to the deck, raced to the hatch, and jumped down, one by one.

"Right full rudder," Reynolds cried.

"Range to escort, two-five-oh-oh."

They heard a third explosion in the convoy. Pierpont saw that they had hit the freighter with the last salvo, and he shouted, "Hits in the freighter."

"Rudder amidship," Reynolds said, looking aft with binoculars at the onrushing destroyer. "I'm going to let him close to two thousand yards and fire nine and ten down the throat."

In the conning tower, Mills experienced a wave of doubt. He fought an urge to run to the bridge and take over. A down-the-throat shot was a good tactic in theory. At the officers' club bar, anyway. The theory was that when the destroyer saw the oncoming torpedoes, she would turn port or starboard to get out of the way and catch the torpedoes broadside. But what if she didn't see the torpedoes, or what if she continued on a straight course, presenting the smallest possible target? *Shark* was certain to miss and be rammed and sunk. Only a few skippers in the submarine force had ever had the guts to fire down the throat. It was like playing Russian roulette. But this was Mike's game now, his call.

"Okay, Mike," said Mills, clenching his fists.

"Crazy son of a bitch," Pierpont said under his breath. "He's going for all the marbles first time out."

Pierpont didn't hear the incoming shell. It exploded off the port beam, and the concussion threw him and Reynolds to the deck. Pierpont was stunned, momentarily unable to move. Then he rose shakily to his knees and saw that Reynolds was out cold, sprawled on the deck grotesquely. He crawled to Reynolds and propped him erect. Then he felt the warm liquid on Reynolds's shirt front, and he shouted at the intercom, "The exec's hit!"

# CHAPTER THREE

Mills bulled his way to the bridge ladder. By the time he got there, Pierpont was lowering Reynolds, who was still unconscious and bloody. Mills caught the limp body and shouted up the hatch, "Clear the bridge! Dive! Dive!" and Pierpont jumped down the hatch, pulling it shut by the lanyard. The helmsman, Frank Nalle, stepped over and dogged it. Mills lowered Reynolds through the hatch to the control room. The pharmacist's mate, Roger Jones, left his post at the sonar gear to minister to him. Pierpont took over sonar.

The diving Klaxon blasted twice: *Aauuuugah. Aauuuugah.* Throughout the boat, skilled hands moved quickly to change *Shark* from a diesel-powered surface vessel to a battery-powered submerged vessel. Diesel engines stopped. Main induction and all hull openings were shut. Main vents were opened. Bow planes were rigged out. Radar and radio were secured.

The chief of the boat, Archie Wheeler, a pot-bellied old salt universally known as Pops, stood at his post in the control room, just forward of the diving plane wheels. He faced a panel of lights called the Christmas tree. The lights on the panel were shifting from red to green as the hull openings were shut, and when all the lights were green, he reported, "Green board!"

*Shark* was now theoretically watertight. To be sure of that, Wheeler ordered a machinist at the air manifold to bleed high-pressure air into the boat. It came in with a brief earsplitting hiss. Wheeler's eyes were fixed on a gauge similar to an aircraft altimeter. The needle swung, reflecting the increase of pressure, and when it held, indicating that *Shark* was indeed airtight and therefore watertight, Wheeler reported, "Pressure in the boat."

*Shark* nosed down. From the conning tower, Mills ordered, "Make the depth four hundred feet. Fifteen degrees down bubble. Rig for depth charge. Rig for silent running."

*Shark* "hung" momentarily at thirty-six feet, then plunged steeply. Fifty seconds after Mills had given the order to dive, she was completely submerged and rapidly gaining downward speed. It was eerily quiet.

At his post before the sonar stack in the conning

tower, Pierpont adjusted the sound level of the passive listening gear and searched 360 degrees. There was noise all over the dial: the hideous hiss and crash of the torpedoed ships breaking up and sinking; the dull *thump-thump* of the other merchant ship screws; the *whir* of the high-speed escort screws. He found the destroyer and reported, "High-speed screws at two-five-oh. Short-scale pinging." The destroyer was close, echo-ranging, preparing to depth charge.

"Right full rudder," Mills ordered, eyes on the needle of the depth gauge: 150 feet; 200 . . . 250 . . . 300. Then, "All ahead emergency." The pitlog edged to 8.5 knots.

Pierpont fixed the sound gear on the destroyer. Nothing else mattered for the moment. Nothing in the world.

"Left full rudder," Mills said. "Steady as you go." He was twisting and turning, seeking to confuse the Japanese sonar operators, searching for a thermocline—a cold layer of water that would distort the destroyer's electronic ping and give a false position of the submarine.

Suddenly Pierpont detected a slight change in the destroyer's screw cavitation. *Shark* was swinging; that might be expected. He zeroed in on the destroyer's bearing. No. There was something odd. It seemed to be turning away. He tracked it with mounting disbelief. Then, when he was absolutely certain, he reported, "Destroyer turning away!"

"What?" Mills said. He squeezed his way through the men to the sound stack and put one earphone to his ear. It was true. The high-speed screws could be heard only faintly. They were definitely drawing away.

"Well, I'm damned," Mills said, returning the earphones to Pierpont. He lifted his baseball cap and scratched his thinning, closely cropped blond hair. "I'll never understand those bastards. He had us dead to rights. Then he buzzes off."

"They're unionized," Al Weir said. "It's time for their coffee break."

Mills stared at Weir for a moment. He respected Weir. He was the best radar technician in the sub force, but he was a smart ass. He never speculated, never asked questions. He just gave answers. His jokes were lousy, feeble. With difficulty, Mills disguised his feelings. "Not a bad idea, Weir. Let's take a break ourselves."

He turned to Bell. "Take the conn, Jim. Secure from battle stations. Secure from silent running. Set the watch. But keep her deep for a while, just in case. Steer due east, full speed."

As Mills lowered himself down the ladder to the control room, Bell's voice could be heard on the PA system, securing from the emergency and resetting the normal twelve-to-four watch. Mills paused a moment to give Pops Wheeler and the others in the control room a "well-done." Then he continued on to the forward battery compartment, adroitly stepping through the small opening of the massive steel watertight doorway.

The forward battery was chief petty officer and officer country. The five chiefs had their own small compartment at the rear. Opposite that was a small captain's cabin, Mills's private and personal domain. It was about the size of a Pullman car roomette with a bunk, a stainless steel sink, a head, and a safe that held highly classified material—such as the code books and strip ciphers. The other officers shared the small compartments along the passageway, two or three to a room. Beneath the deck of this compartment was one-half of *Shark*'s battery, 125 huge cells.

Mills pulled aside the wardroom curtain and peered in. Doc Jones had laid the unconscious Mike Reynolds out on the wardroom dining table, which occupied almost the whole of that space. He had cut away his bloody shirt and trousers, administered morphine, and rigged a blood plasma bottle. One of the two mess stewards, José

Martinez, a Filipino, held the plasma bottle aloft while Doc probed the stomach wound with forceps.

"How is he?" Mills asked.

"Not good," Jones said without looking up. "Deep internal wounds. Hemorrhaging. He's lost a lot of blood."

It seemed unbelievable to Mills that it had happened at all. Submariners were rarely injured like this.

"Can you handle it?"

"I'll do my best, captain," Jones said as he clamped a blood vessel, "but if we don't get him to a hospital, he's going to die."

Mills considered where to go. It would have to be Majuro Atoll. The island had recently been taken from the Japanese as part of the Marshall Islands invasion operations, and the roadstead was being converted to a fleet anchorage. Vice Admiral Charles A. Lockwood, Jr., commander submarines Pacific Fleet, had established an advance headquarters there in the submarine tender *Holland*, which had superb medical facilities, but it was 1,600 nautical miles away; a four-day voyage at full speed.

"Our best bet is Majuro," said Mills. "Four days. Can he last that long?"

Doc Jones looked up wearily. "You want my honest opinion?"

"Yes. Of course."

"I doubt it. It depends on many intangibles—his constitutional strength, his will to live . . ."

"Is there anything I can do?" Mills asked.

"I'll need whole blood," Jones said. "Type O. Pints and pints."

"You'll have it," Mills said, rolling up his sleeve. "Starting with me."

# CHAPTER FOUR

*Shark* picked up her escort fifty miles north-west of Majuro. It was a destroyer escort, the *Ralph D. Harrison*. Three hours later, they could see the low atoll from *Shark*'s bridge, and one hour later they passed through the open submarine net and entered the anchorage.

Mills took the conn. He was dressed in clean, pressed khakis and a brand-new red baseball cap. The cap was strictly against regulations, but it was a Mills trademark, a distinctive touch the admiral himself had authorized.

Pierpont came on the bridge dressed in clean dungarees.

"Good morning, captain. Permission to rig for port?"

"Good morning, Bob," Mills said, grinning broadly and lighting up a cigar. "Permission granted."

Pierpont had the new quartermaster, Jack Childress, in tow. Childress was laden with a heavy canvas bag.

Pierpont said, "Okay, string 'em up."

Childress climbed into the periscope shears and opened the bag. It contained a long white line, to which small flags were attached. White flags with a red ball in the center represented Japanese merchantmen sunk; white flags with fanlike red rays represented Japanese men-of-war sunk. Childress fixed one end of the line to number one periscope, then scrambled down to the deck and secured the other end to a cleat on the bow. It was

15

an impressive display; thirty ships in all, five men-of-war and twenty-five merchant ships. No other boat could claim so many sinkings. Three of the flags were brand-new, representing the three ships sunk by Mike Reynolds on this patrol. All hands regarded the display with immense pride.

Pierpont said to the captain, "How's Mr. Reynolds?"

"No change," Mills said.

"How's Doc?"

"Dead on his feet," Mills said.

"Good man," Pierpont said. "Anybody else would have lost him."

"I'm putting you and Doc in for Bronze Stars," Mills said.

Pierpont was inwardly overjoyed, but he parried, "Why me? I didn't do anything."

"You were on the bridge during the gun attack," Mills said, mentally composing the citation. "With fearless disregard for your own safety, you lowered the wounded exec to the conning tower, thereby saving his life."

"Captain, I was just trying to save my own ass."

"Nine out of ten medals are awarded for that reason," Mills said. "Including mine." He turned to the intercom. "Station the maneuvering watch."

The line handlers came on deck dressed in clean dungarees and white hats. They rigged steel cable lifelines and got the heaving lines ready.

Pierpont fixed his binoculars on a nest of auxiliary vessels anchored in the far end of the lagoon. "There's the *Holland*," he said.

"Where away?" Mills said.

"Dead ahead," Pierpont replied. "She's signaling us."

"Man the signal light," said Mills.

Pierpont climbed up in the shears, aimed the light, and blinked out a "go ahead." He read the reply from *Holland* with difficulty, for he got little blinker light practice on *Shark*, but finally he made it out and reported to Mills, "Medical personnel standing by. Moor portside."

"Very well," Mills said.

"There was an unofficial postscript," Pierpont said. "The admiral flew in this morning."

"Lockwood?"

"Yes, sir."

They steamed up the lagoon at slow speed. It was a beautiful tropical atoll, still intact. Palm trees. White sand beaches. Clear, placid, azure waters. Mills concluded—correctly, as it turned out—that the marines had taken the atoll without a fight.

They approached *Holland*, a majestic lady in the sub force named for a mad engineer named John P. Holland who sold the navy its first submarine in 1900. Mills had served on her staff briefly in 1938, before he was assigned to *Pike*.

*Holland*'s portside was clear, so *Shark* could nest directly alongside. Her band had gathered on the stern for the traditional welcome. Amidships, a knot of white-coated medical personnel were waiting with a stretcher, and on the port bridge wing, Mills saw a group of navy brass, including Admiral Lockwood; his towering chief of staff, Sunshine Murray; and his operations officer, Dick Voge. Lockwood waved affably. Mills saluted across the water and held up three fingers for the three ships sunk. Lockwood clenched his hands over his head like a triumphant prizefighter. Nothing pleased him more than a "good bag."

Mills brought the boat in smoothly and easily. The lines went across, then the brow, and the band saluted them with a stirring march. The first men across the brow were the medical personnel—two doctors, three corpsmen, and two stretcher-bearers. Mills met them on deck and escorted them to the wardroom.

Mike Reynolds had regained consciousness on the second day after he was wounded. Nursed along by Doc Jones, he had remained alive, then recovered—to a point, but Doc still considered him critical. Mike smiled at the *Holland* doctor and at Mills standing behind him, and he said weakly, "Hell of a way to arrive in port, captain." He was transferred to the stretcher, bound in tightly, and vertically lifted up the forward torpedo room hatch.

On deck, he managed a weak salute to Mills. "Permission to go ashore, captain?"

"Granted," Mills said, feeling a deep emotional tremor. He knelt at the stretcher and took Reynolds's hand in his. "A hell of an attack," he said. "Very, very gutsy."

"I had a gutsy teacher," Reynolds said, "but I guess I flunked the course."

"The hell you did," Mills protested. "You passed with honors. As soon as you're back on your feet, you'll get your own boat."

"I'm going to miss this boat, Jack," Reynolds said, closing his eyes. "I grew up here."

"We all did a little growing up here," said Mills.

As they carried Reynolds across the bow, Mills called out, "Attention on deck," and his order was echoed the length of the boat. He stood ramrod straight and saluted, and all hands on deck followed his example. As he saluted from the bridge, Quartermaster Pierpont thought, Reynolds is a shit, but he's our shit, and he'll be damned difficult to replace.

# CHAPTER FIVE

Captain Mills put on his regulation khaki hat with the scrambled eggs on the bill, picked up a brown envelope containing *Shark*'s lengthy typed patrol report, and went topside. By now, *Holland* personnel had brought aboard the mail, fresh fruit, and milk, and half of *Shark*'s enlisted personnel were lounging on deck eating apples and oranges and reading two month's accumulation of letters from home. Jim Bell and the other subordinate officers were conferring with the officers from *Holland*'s relief crew who would take charge of the boat for the next two weeks while *Shark* personnel blew off steam at the Majuro submarine rest camp.

Mills found Admiral Lockwood in the flag officers' dining room, a small space on *Holland* reserved for special occasions such as this one. It had become a sub force tradition that the admiral and his chief of staff had lunch with skippers returning from patrol. The lunch was considered informal and off the record, and the admiral learned more about the patrol—and the skipper—than he ever would from the formal patrol report.

A Filipino mess steward in whites stood by as Lockwood and Murray invited Mills to be seated.

"Would you like steak or turkey?" Lockwood asked.

"Steak, sir," Mills responded, and while the steward went off to prepare the lunch, Mills studied the admiral. A genial, thoughtful, fair-minded man, he was respectfully known among the sub skippers as Uncle Charlie. Not a brilliant student or tactician, but a genius at handling people. Curiously, Murray was cut from the same cloth: affable, always optimistic (hence, Sunshine), evenhanded. The real brains—the strategist at SubPac—was Lockwood's operations officer, Dick Voge.

"The medics say Reynolds is going to be all right," Lockwood said. "Your pharmacist did a splendid job. You should put him in for a gong."

"I will," Mills said. "And a promotion to chief."

Lockwood turned to Murray. "See that it's put through immediately." Then, to Mills, "How did it happen?"

Mills recounted in detail the attack on the convoy, and both men registered surprise when they learned that Mills had turned the command over to Reynolds.

"I'm not sure I approve of that," said Lockwood.

"Put it this way, admiral," Mills rejoined, "Mike is qualified for command. You give him a boat. He goes on patrol. He makes his first attack—all alone. In this case, I was there if anything went wrong. As it happened, plenty went wrong. It seems to me it's a better way for new skippers to break the ice."

"I think so, too, admiral," said Sunshine Murray. "It ought to be standard procedure for prospective commanding officers."

"But how many skippers would go along with that policy?" said Lockwood. "Most would want the kills for themselves. Kills don't grow on trees, you know. Kills mean medals. Medals mean promotions."

They kicked the idea around for another ten minutes, reaching no firm conclusion, and then the steward served lunch.

Mills said to Lockwood, "Sir, I recommend Reynolds for his own command."

Lockwood sipped his milk thoughtfully. "I'm

not sure I want to drop to the class of '37. Nor am I quite certain about Reynolds. I don't really approve of down-the-throat shots, surface or submerged."

"It was a gutsy call," said Mills.

"He came close to losing the boat," said Lockwood. "I'm not sure you did the right thing either."

If Lockwood—and his staff—had a fault, Mills thought, it was excessive caution about losses. Too much emphasis on bringing the boat back. Hell, there's a war on.

Lockwood read his mind. "This war's not going to be won in a week—or a month. It'll take another two years, at least. We don't need brash heroics. We need steady, relentless pressure applied in a cool, methodical manner." He paused to fold his linen napkin and insert it in a silver ring that was decorated with a three-star insignia. Then he said, "Your patrol will be judged successful for award of the Submarine Combat Insignia. The three ships Reynolds sank will earn you another Navy Cross. Congratulations."

As he stood to leave, Lockwood gave Mills a warm handshake. "I wish I had about a dozen more skippers like you."

Murray shook his hand and said, "This is a damned fine relief crew, Jack. They'll give you all the support you folks need. If not, give me a holler."

When Mills returned to *Shark*, he was mildly confused; he wasn't sure whether he was on the admiral's shit list or what. Maybe that's how you got flag rank. You learned to talk out of both sides of your mouth at once—in circles.

# CHAPTER SIX

The Majuro Officers' Club stood on a sandy rise facing the lagoon. Mills and Jim Bell took a table outside on the wooden deck, and a steward brought scotch for Mills, bourbon for Bell. It was a lovely tropical evening.

That week the Majuro lagoon had been officially named a Pacific Fleet anchorage. It was now occupied by Admiral Raymond Spruance's vast Fifth Fleet, just returned from a carrier attack on Guam and Saipan islands. Countless ships rode at anchor: carriers, battleships, heavy and light cruisers, destroyers, fleet tankers. Mills and Bell gawked at the sight as they sipped their drinks. Neither had ever seen such an awesome display of naval power.

"Do you know Admiral Spruance?" Bell asked.

"Yes," Mills said. "I met him when I was a plebe."

"What's he like?"

"Scholarly," Mills said. "An intellectual. Probably the best-read admiral in the navy. Very conservative at sea. Not my kind of admiral. I'll take Bull Halsey any day. That's what we need to win this war. Bull Halsey in the top command."

Just as Mills lifted his empty glass toward a steward for a refill, there was an explosion in the lagoon. Flames were shooting a thousand feet into the air, and Mills and Bell jumped up and raced to the railing. Officers poured out of the club, babbling excitedly.

"A ship blew up!" shouted Mills.

"Which one?" an officer asked.

"Don't know," Mills said.

An air-raid siren wailed. In the lagoon, ships signaled back and forth frantically and got up steam.

"Come on, Jim," said Mills. "Let's get down to the boat."

They raced to the jeep, a loaner from SubPac, and Mills careened along the road to the fleet landing where dozens of liberty launches were mooring and departing in haste, picking up officers and sailors to return to their ships. They recognized a gig from the *Holland*, leaped aboard, and five minutes later they reached the tender, which was on full alert and making up steam.

They raced up the starboard gangway, crossed over the *Holland*, and descended the bow to the nest of submarines on the portside. *Shark* was moored outboard of *Silverfish* and *Seadragon*, both undergoing refit and not capable of getting under way. *Shark*, freshly refitted and sporting a new gray and black camouflage paint job, was on full alert. Mills hurried to the bridge, shouting orders to prepare to get under way.

Pierpont was on the bridge, holding binoculars and a megaphone for Mills. "What the hell's going on, sir?"

"Don't know," said Mills. "One of those ships blew sky-high." He shouted into the megaphone to the deck gang, "Single up all lines." Then to the intercom, "All four engines on the line." Black smoke belched from the four engine exhaust ports as the machinists fired up the diesels.

Pierpont trained his binoculars on Spruance's flagship, a battlewagon, and read her signal blinker aloud. "To all small boys. Enemy submarine believed to have pen—didn't get that word, captain —lagoon. Stop. Small boys hunt and kill."

*"Penetrated*, you dummy," Mills said, a trifle irked. "Submarine penetrated the lagoon. We're

going to have to send you back to blinker school, Pierpont. Signal the flagship: *Shark* joining small boys for surface search."

"Aye, aye," said Pierpont, feeling not a little chagrined that his captain could read blinker better than he.

"Cast off all lines!" Mills shouted. Then to the intercom, "All back one-third."

*Shark* pulled away from *Holland* into the deep lagoon, threading through the mass of moored ships, all active and passive sonar manned.

"It was a battlewagon—the *Florida*," said Pierpont, still attempting to read the flagship blinker. "Went down with all hands."

"Wonder how the hell a submarine got through the net," Mills mused aloud. "Somebody dropped the ball. Well, she can't get out, that's for sure."

Within a half hour, upward of fifty destroyers and *Shark* were stalking the lagoon. The flotilla hunted all through the night, the following day, and the following night, but not a trace of the enemy submarine was ever found. It simply was not there. The court of inquiry appointed to investigate the cause of the disaster was eventually forced to rule "Unknown. Probably an accidental internal explosion."

# CHAPTER SEVEN

A messenger arrived at *Shark* with the news that Admiral Lockwood wished to see Commander Mills at once. Mills found Lockwood in his commodious office on *Holland*'s boat deck. The room was decorated with photographs of ancient boats

Lockwood had commanded in World War I and during the twenties: *A-2, B-1, G-1, N-5, R-25, S-14,* and the big fleet boat *V-3,* also known as *Bonita.*

"Have a seat, Mills," said Lockwood without looking up from the pile of paperwork on his desk. After a time, he gave Mills his attention. "I think Dick Voge has solved your exec problem." He paused to use the ship's telephone. "Have Captain Voge come to my office, please."

Almost immediately, Dick Voge entered the open door, and Mills jumped up to shake hands. They were old friends, for Mills had been engineering officer on Voge's *Sealion* in 1940. Voge laid a manila folder on the admiral's desk. It was tabbed *Hunt, Wm. C.*

Voge said to Lockwood, "Hunt's been bugging me for sea duty for months, and he's earned it."

"Can you really spare him?" Lockwood asked.

"Yes. Joe Grenfell's working in very nicely."

"All right by me, then," said Lockwood.

Voge passed the folder to Mills, and when Mills glanced at the résumé, his eyes fell immediately on one line: "Postgraduate degree: Law."

"A lawyer!" he said. "You're sending me to sea with a lawyer? Good God, Dick!"

"Now wait a minute." Voge was bristling. "He's fully qualified for submarines." Voge may have been brilliant, but he had a notoriously quick temper.

Mills studied the résumé. "He hasn't been on a fleet boat—or any boat at all—since 1940!"

Seeking support, Voge glanced at Lockwood.

"He's damned good," said Lockwood. "The best man I could offer you. I suggest you have a talk with him, and you'll see what I mean."

Mills found Hunt in his stateroom in the staff officers' quarters. He looked like Mills's idea of a lawyer: not very tall, dark hair, olive skin, horn-rimmed glasses. They shook hands.

"You know why I'm here?" Mills asked.

"Yes. Have a chair."

Mills sat down. "What'd you do at the Academy?"

"*Lucky Bag* and *Wave*, the literary magazine,' Hunt said.

"I mean sports," said Mills.

"Fencing."

"Fencing?" Mills snorted. "Fencing!"

"And crew," Hunt said. "Coxswain."

"Well, that's a little better," Mills said grudgingly.

"I was too small for contact sports," Hunt offered.

"A lawyer, eh?" said Mills. "What kind of lawyer?"

"Contract law," Hunt said.

"Contract law!" Mills snorted again. "What do you know about fighting submarines?"

"I graduated number one in my sub school class," Hunt said, "then did a year and a half on *Pickerel* as assistant engineering officer. I qualified. When Pearl Harbor came, I was stuck in Harvard Law School. Then I did a stint in the inspector general's office. When I asked to return to submarine sea duty, my request was granted, but then Captain Voge shanghaied me to his staff."

"Why?"

"We're old family friends," Hunt said. "My uncle and his dad were law partners in Boston."

"I see." Mills was silent for a moment, mulling over this impossible situation. Then he said, "Okay, Hunt. You're at four hundred feet. You lose all power, all air systems. You can't make any turns. You can't blow. How do you get up?"

Hunt thought a moment, taking off his glasses. "There's a way. Laborious, but it would work. You hand-crank the periscopes up. Fully extend them. The periscopes will displace water. Not much, but some. Your displacement is now greater for the same weight, giving you, by Archimedes' law, positive buoyancy. So the boat will rise, very gradually and very slowly."

Mills stared at Hunt, much impressed. He glanced at his watch. "Let's go over to the O Club and have a drink."

# CHAPTER EIGHT

Dick Voge summoned Mills to his operations office at 0715. Mills had a monstrous hangover. He had consumed a Niagara of scotch before he decided he was willing to give Bill Hunt a shot as exec of *Shark*. They had had no dinner.

Voge, eyeing his old friend, said, "I hope you got his license number."

"Whose license number?"

"The truck that hit you."

"Aw, shit, Dick. I'm *supposed* to be blowing off steam."

Voge was not one for small talk. Handing Mills a manila folder, he said, "Have a look at this."

Inside, there was a memorandum stamped *Ultra Secret*. That stamp, Mills knew, was reserved exclusively for material emanating from the U.S. Navy's Japanese code breakers. The memorandum was brief:

ALL I-CLASS JAP SUBS HAVE BEEN ORDERED TO REPORT TO YOKOSUKA NAVAL BASE OUTSIDE TOKYO. REASON NOT KNOWN.

Mills returned the folder. "Interesting," he said.

"Yes, very," Voge replied. "Nothing like it ever happened before."

"Have any ideas?"

"Nothing worthwhile. Best we can figure is they must have some new gear they want to retrofit."

"But all the boats at once?" said Mills.

"It does seem unlikely," Voge conceded. "Unless, of course, it's something really vital and revolutionary. And that's what we want *Shark* to find out. On your next patrol, you'll reconnoiter Yokosuka."

"Are you nuts?" Mills exploded. "You can't get into Tokyo Bay. They've got the whole Jap navy in there, not to mention the submarine net."

"Some time ago, your new exec submitted a staff proposal regarding that net," said Voge as he passed Mills another folder. "I think it's fairly ingenious."

Mills scanned the *Top Secret* memorandum inside the folder. It was labeled *Tokyo Bay Submarine Net, Penetration of*. In essence, the plan submitted by Bill Hunt was simple: slip into the bay beneath a large ingoing vessel. The technical backup was long and impressively detailed. Mills returned the folder without comment.

"Feasible?" Voge asked.

"It looks good on paper," Mills said. "All plans look good on paper. It's the real thing that causes problems. But, Dick, why me? You know I *hate* these special missions. They're usually nonproductive. What I'm good at is sinking ships."

"Actually, you weren't our first choice, Jack," Voge said. "The admiral held out for someone with a little more, ah, finesse. But when we sent Hunt to you, *Shark* seemed a logical choice, since the whole scheme is Hunt's and he's studied it thoroughly."

Miller appraised Voge carefully. "They say you were an Armenian rug merchant before you went to the Academy. I think it's true. You really set me up, didn't you?"

Voge laughed. "Sure, Jack. I foresaw that Mike

would be wounded, that you would need a new exec, and—"

"All right. Knock it off. I know when I've been had."

Mills rose to leave. "I can wheel and deal, too, captain. If I do this for you, you do something for me. See that Mike gets his own command."

"He'll get a command."

"The admiral didn't seem to think so."

"Where'd you get the idea that the admiral runs the sub force?" Voge said, winking. "By the way, I think Hunt will be an asset for you. You need a balance wheel, Jack. A foil. He'll be a good one."

"I don't know about that," said Mills, "but I'm willing to give it a try for one run. Then we'll see. Lawyers make me nervous."

## CHAPTER NINE

The Majuro NCO Club was only slightly less elegant than the officers' club. It, too, occupied a sandy knoll overlooking the lagoon. The big difference was that the NCO club was not authorized to serve hard alcohol. Only beer.

Bob Pierpont and his protégé, Jack Childress, arrived at the club near sunset. Pierpont had a flask in the hip pocket of his dungarees, and the flask was filled with "gilly," or "pink lady"— torpedo propellant alcohol swiped from *Shark*'s torpedo room. The alcohol had been distilled and was safe to drink. It was 180 proof.

Pierpont and Childress chose a table beneath a glassless picture window overlooking the lagoon.

The table was crowded with empty beer pitchers, dirty glasses, and overflowing ashtrays, and while Childress cleared off the table, Pierpont bought a pitcher of beer and borrowed two jiggers from the bartender.

"Have you ever had a depth charge?" Pierpont asked Childress.

"No. What's that?"

"It's a drink the sub force invented."

Pierpont poured two glasses of beer and filled the two jiggers with torpedo alcohol from the flask. He carefully picked up one jigger between his thumb and forefinger, held it over the glass of beer, and let it fall into the glass. Then he raised the glass and sipped.

"A depth charge," he said, grinning. "You'll see. It'll hit you like one."

Childress dropped the jigger into his glass and drank. Liquid fire ran down his throat, and it was all he could do to suppress a cry of pain. His face turned red, his eyes watered, and Pierpont nearly broke up laughing.

They drank one depth charge, then two more. During the last, Pops Wheeler, the chief of the boat, came in and sat down. He was smoking a giant cigar. "Did you guys get the word? Our new exec—Mr. Hunt—is a fucking legal eagle. He hasn't been on a boat since 1940."

Pierpont thought that was riotous. Everything now struck him as hilarious. Wheeler shrugged and poured himself a glass of beer. Childress was fascinated by Pop's tattoos. Both exposed arms were dense with art, and Childress studied the art woozily.

Wheeler said to Childress, "Well, you got your combat pin on your first run. Things have sure changed." And to Pierpont, "It took us a long, long time, didn't it?"

"As we say in Brisbane, too right, old chap," said Pierpont.

"Why?" Childress asked.

Wheeler took the floor. It was his favorite subject. "Before the war, BuOrd—the Bureau of Ordnance—came out to Pearl, swore us to secrecy, and told us they had this awesome new naval weapon. *Awesome* was the word this BuOrd captain used. A magnetic exploder for the Mark 14 torpedo. Didn't have to hit the target. Just get under it. The ship's magnetic field would explode the torpedo beneath the ship. All the Jap battlewagons have armor plating on the side, you see, to ward off torpedoes. But not *underneath*. Now we would be able to break the backbone of a battlewagon with these fabulous fish. Well, to make a long story short, the fucking gadget didn't work. And BuOrd wouldn't believe us. They said we weren't shooting straight, and those stubborn assholes sent us to war with defective torpedoes. A long time went by before gutsy skippers like Mills got command and proved the torpedoes were defective. BuOrd finally conceded reluctantly that they had been true assholes, but in the meantime a lot of good men died, and it took a long time before the sub force started sinking ships."

"And getting combat pins for doing it," Pierpont put in.

"How long was the boat based in Australia?" Childress said, bored with the subject of old torpedoes. They worked fine now.

"I'm glad you asked that question," Pierpont returned. "Twelve months! Twelve heavenly months. Pops, you remember how I connected with Alice? Good old Alice?"

"No," Wheeler said. "How?" He knew, of course. He'd heard it ten times. But he loved the story and wanted to hear it again.

"Beautiful chick," Pierpont said, directing the story to Childress. "Nineteen. Built like a brick shithouse. Well, one day we were coming up the river in Brisbane to New Farm Wharf. I had the watch. I look over on the bank and see someone

madly flailing semaphore flags. Well, my semaphore is a little rusty, right? I mean, you don't
get much semaphore practice on a submerged
submarine, but I grab my flags and give the
guy a 'go ahead.' Would you believe—this is not
a guy? This is Alice! She'd learned semaphore
in order to connect with the U.S. Navy."

He laughed heartily. Wheeler, anticipating, also
laughed, and goaded, "Go on—go on." '

"Well, I connected with Alice. Man, she was—
well . . . use your imagination. Now it developed
that Alice had a sister a couple years older, who
came home from Sydney. Patricia. Even better
built than Alice. She got hot to trot, so I had to
drop Alice temporarily and take Patricia out.
That was going along fine when who should show
up but the mother. She'd been on holiday in
Cairns. Well, Jack, you should have seen the
mother! Carol. A classic beauty. Classic!"

He paused to sip his depth charge. Wheeler
was beside himself. "Go on. Go on!"

"All right." Pierpont resumed. "She must have
married this guy—bloke—when she was fourteen or something because she was mid-thirties
at the most. He died in Changi. That's a Jap POW
camp in Singapore. Well, Carol was horny beyond
belief. Couldn't keep her hands off me. Right?"

"Too right!" Wheeler put in with relish.

Pierpont frowned gravely. "Then the trouble
started. First we find out Alice is knocked up.
Jesus! Then Patricia gets knocked up. Jesus Christ!
Then Carol gets knocked up. Jesus H. Christ! Nobody knows what to do. I mean, down there, they
never even heard of abortion, right?"

"Too right," Wheeler put in, on the verge of
breaking up.

"The mother panicked," said Pierpont. "She
came down and saw the Old Man—the captain.
Asked him what the U.S. Navy was going to do
about it. The Old Man called me in and said,
'Well, Pierpont, in my eight years in the navy,

I've never seen anything like this. What are you going to do?' I said, 'Well, I don't know what to do, sir.' And the Old Man said, 'You're going to have to get married.' And I said, knees slamming, 'To which one, sir?' And he said, 'To the senior one of course. The mother—Carol.' I said, 'But, sir, what about Alice and Patricia?' He said I'd have to take care of them all. Plus the three babies. He'd arrange a transfer to shore duty in Brisbane. Talk about scared shitless!"

Pierpont laughed. Wheeler guffawed. Childress was awestruck.

"Go on—go on," Wheeler managed.

"The Old Man says—he was very serious—he says, 'Pierpont, your situation is unique. After you marry the mother, and the daughters give birth, the babies will be your children and your grandchildren all at once! And your baby by Carol will be the halfbrother or -sister of Alice and Patricia. And—' Well, you know, he let me hang for three days? The day we sailed, he called me down again. He says, 'Pierpont, is your gear all packed?' I said, sweating, 'Yes, sir. All packed.' He let me stand there about five minutes, sweating and quaking. Then he picked up my orders and tore them up. He said, 'Pierpont, I'm going to do you a big favor. I'm going to take you back to the war zone where you'll be safe.' "

Pierpont and Wheeler convulsed. After he stopped laughing, Childress tried to bring his mind together and sort out what the family relationship would have been had Pierpont married Carol. It was beyond his comprehension.

"The Old Man's all heart," Pierpont managed.

"All heart!" Wheeler echoed, breaking up again.

A submarine sailor with a menacing look in his eye strolled over from the bar. He said to Pierpont, "You guys off the *Shark?*"

Pierpont had seen that look before. "What's it to you, Mac? Shove off."

"I hear your Old Man chickened out and the

exec had to make the attack," the sailor said, almost jeering.

Pierpont and Wheeler were on their feet in a split second. Pierpont grabbed the sailor by his dungaree shirt and hit him harder than Childress had ever seen a man hit. The sailor reeled back, falling over a table, and beer pitchers, glasses, and ashtrays scattered to the floor. Two other sailors helped their shipmate to his feet. Then all three charged, fists flying.

# CHAPTER TEN

Jack Mills, Bill Hunt, and Jim Bell stood at the bar of the officers' club sipping highballs and playing liar's dice for the check. Above the hubbub a steward shouted, "Commander Mills, phone call! Commander Mills, phone call!"

Mills went to the telephone. "Mills here."

"Captain," said an urgent voice, "this is Seaman Nalle, topside watch, sir."

"Yes. What is it, Nalle?"

"Sir, we just got a call from the NCO club. Er, sir, Chief Wheeler and Pierpont and some of the guys are cleaning house, sir. The SPs are on the way."

Mills slammed the phone in its cradle and rushed back to the bar. "Come on, Mr. Hunt. You're about to meet the best damn crew in this fighting man's navy."

They raced for the jeep and piled in, Mills at the wheel, driving wildly. In three minutes, they reached the NCO club driveway and screeched to a halt in the sand alongside two SP jeeps.

Mills tore up the walkway, mounted the steps three at a time, and yanked open the door, Hunt and Bell right behind him.

His mouth agape, Mills paused a second in the doorway. It was an all-out riot: twenty or thirty submarine sailors throwing punches, a half dozen SPs with billy sticks futilely trying to break it up. Mills saw Chief Wheeler, back against the wall, taking it in his big gut.

"I'm coming, Pops!" cried Mills, plunging into the melee, half blind with rage, ruthlessly pushing and shoving men aside.

An SP loomed in the captain's path, shouting, "Get out, sir! We'll handle this," and Mills shot the SP an angry look of disbelief and roughly knocked him aside. In three more strides, he reached the sailor who was assaulting Wheeler, threw a lock around his neck from behind, pounded him in the side until he felt the man go limp, and dropped him to the floor.

Wheeler was bruised, bleeding, and gasping. He looked around, shouted to Mills, "Pierpont and Childress," and Mills and Wheeler plunged back into the melee, shoving and punching until they found their two shipmates backed into a corner by four sailors. Mills took two, Wheeler two, and all four went down.

"Come on," Mills shouted to his men, "let's get the hell out of here."

The three men, led by Mills, ran for the door, and at the same moment a dozen new SPs, a lieutenant in the lead, rushed into the room blowing whistles, wielding, sticks, blocking the door. It was all over in a moment. The NCO club was an utter shambles.

"Arrest all hands," commanded the SP lieutenant. He looked up, saw Mills, and said, "What are you doing here?"

"Getting my men out," Mills said.

One of the SPs walked up and said in a surly tone, "Lieutenant, the commander here struck an enlisted man. Three, in fact. I saw him do it with my own eyes."

The lieutenant addressed Mills. "Is that true, commander?"

"Yes, that's true."

"You're under arrest," the lieutenant said.

Bill Hunt and Jim Bell pushed through the crowd, and Hunt drew Mills aside and said in a low but authoritative tone, "Don't say another goddamn word. Let me handle it." Mills looked at his exec, dumbfounded.

Hunt turned to the SP lieutenant and said icily, "Lieutenant Bell and I witnessed the entire episode. Your men had obviously lost control of the situation. Under *Navy Regulations*, article twenty-one, subsection sixteen Baker, as amended, the commander was fully within his rights. The statute states in part that, quote, when an uncontrollable mutiny or uprising is clearly in evidence, the commanding officer is authorized to take whatever action is necessary, including the use of physical force, to protect the lives and welfare of those personnel remaining loyal to him, unquote." He paused to let that sink in, then added, "Quite clearly—owing to the ineffectiveness of your own men—the situation was uncontrollable."

Mills stared in amazement at his exec.

The SP lieutenant was flustered, yet unbowed. "He struck an enlisted man. I have an eyewitness."

Hunt retorted with a force and power that astonished everyone. "You're a legal imbecile, lieutenant! Obviously you have not studied the case law on subsection sixteen Baker, as amended!"

The lieutenant flushed. "Sir, I'm not a lawyer."

"But, you're the arresting officer," Hunt bored in. "Surely, you've been briefed on the rights and responsibilities of the defendant?" He suddenly shifted gears. "At exactly what time did you receive a report of a disturbance here?"

The lieutenant, now on the defensive, said, "At 1920, sir."

"Exactly what was reported to you?"

"That a fight had broken out at the NCO club."

"Those exact words?"

"No, sir."

"What, then?"

"That, er, that they were tearing the place apart, or words to that effect."

"And what was your response?"

"I sent six men. Immediately."

"Six men?" Hunt sneered. "To quell a riot?"

Hunt turned to Mills. "Commander, if the lieutenant insists on filing charges against you, not only are you fully protected by subsection sixteen Baker, you also would be well advised to cross-file charges against the lieutenant under *Navy Regulations*, article one hundred four, subsection nineteen, as amended: Dereliction of Duty. The lieutenant's response to the alarm was clearly inadequate. Because of his poor judgment, your men were placed in peril and jeopardy."

Mills stammered, "Yes, well, I, er . . ."

The SP lieutenant, shaken, drew Hunt aside. "Sir, I'm not a professional SP. I was drafted out of the transient BOQ for this job. Temporary duty only. I am en route to the States for leave."

Hunt was relentless. "Do you know who that man is? That's John R. Mills."

"Mauler Mills? The sub skipper?" the lieutenant said, awed.

"That's him," Hunt pressed. "His boat leaves for patrol tomorrow." He paused dramatically. "Why don't we call it a Mexican standoff? You collect your men, he'll collect his. I'm sure the *Shark*'s slush fund has enough to cover damages to the club. I'll personally see that it is taken care of."

The lieutenant paused only a moment before extending his hand. "A deal." Hunt shook his hand firmly.

Returning to the fleet landing in the jeep, Mills was unusually silent and thoughtful. It had been a close call, he knew. Very close. Relief of command, a general court-martial. Finally, he spoke. "I'm sure glad you know your Rocks and Shoals, Bill. I don't remember any subsection sixteen Baker or—what was the other one?"

"Article one hundred four, subsection nineteen?"

"Yes," said Mills.

"In point of fact," said Hunt, "I don't believe they exist."

Mills slammed on the brakes, stopping the jeep in the middle of the road. "You mean you made all that up?"

"I'm afraid so, captain."

Mills turned to Jim Bell in the back seat. "He made it all up. Out of whole cloth. Can you beat that, Jim? He made it up!"

Mills began to laugh and shake his head. He restarted the jeep and laughed all the way to the fleet landing.

# CHAPTER ELEVEN

Fifty miles northwest of Majuro, *Shark*'s escort turned back, signaling "Good luck, good hunting, Godspeed," and once more *Shark* was on her own, a lone speck moving slowly northwest on the surface of a vast undulating sun-flecked sea.

Jack Mills, wearing his baseball cap, took his ease on the bridge. He felt like a caged tiger let loose. This was his element. He wasn't cut out for the spit-and-polish bullshit back there: luncheons with admirals, staff politics, the goddamn SPs. A new thought occurred to him. Even with four Navy Crosses, he probably wouldn't do well in the postwar peacetime navy. He was not a paper-pusher; he was a goddamn seaman. A simple fighting seaman. This command would be the high point of his career. In a sense, he wished the war would go on forever, just so he could avoid the hell of a letdown he knew would happen when it was all over.

They had entered a submarine safety lane, one of a series of highly classified ocean highways used by the boats going to and from patrol stations. It had been necessary for SubPac to establish these lanes because hair-triggered Allied airmen, unable to distinguish between American and Japanese submarines, attacked either indiscriminately. The lanes had worked—to a point. Allied air attacks on American submarines had diminished significantly, but there were still occasional accidents, so Shark's radar and the bridge watches kept a keen lookout for planes. They would dive to avoid any aircraft.

The twelve-to-four had the watch. Jim Bell, OOD; Childress, quartermaster. Childress was still hung over and bruised, and he had a painful black eye. He wanted nothing more than to fit in with this swashbuckling, devil-may-care crew, but he was damned if he'd ever drink another depth charge. Beer, yes. Gilly, no. Never.

Mills turned to Childress. "How'd the fight start, anyway?"

The question took Childress by surprise. The captain had never spoken directly to him. Now this, of all questions.

"Sir," Childress began, carefully selecting his words, "a sailor came over to our table and made a dirty remark about the boat—about Shark."

"What did he say?"

"I don't know, sir," Childress lied. Better if the Old Man's buddy, Pierpont, or Pops told him. "I was in the head."

Mills spoke into the intercom: "Send Pierpont to the bridge, please."

Pierpont arrived a moment later, his face battered and bruised. Mills looked him over. "You better have Doc take a look at you."

"I did, sir," said Pierpont, speaking with great difficulty through cracked, puffy lips. "It's superficial."

"What started it? What did that sailor say about *Shark?*"

Pierpont glanced at Childress. Good man, he thought. He hadn't given the game away.

"Oh, I dunno," Pierpont said offhandedly. "That we were glory hounds, or something. He was spoiling for a fight."

"Pierpont!" Mills demanded. "Don't lie to me."

Pierpont feigned indignation. "I wouldn't lie to you, captain."

Mills eyed him a moment longer, then said, "Well, thanks for defending the boat's honor."

"Thanks for the rescue."

"I guess we can thank Mr. Hunt," Mills said. "You know it was all bullshit? He made up that legalese about the subsections."

"Most impressive performance I've seen in years," said Pierpont. "The way he turned the tables on that poor slob. In the end, Mr. Hunt was like a prosecutor cross-examining a murder defendant!"

"Aircraft! Bearing one-eight-zero!"

No one even paused to verify the lookout's report. Jim Bell shouted, *"Clear the bridge! Dive. Dive!"* and pushed the bridge diving alarm twice. The three lookouts, and Pierpont and Childress dived for the hatch, Bell counted them aloud. "One. Two. Three. Four. Five. Six." He had never left a man on the bridge.

The vents swooshed open, the bow planes

opened out, the diesels shut down, and the main induction clamped closed with a heavy thump. *Shark* nosed down.

"After you, captain," Bell offered. He didn't want 220 pounds of Jack Mills riding his shoulders down the ladder.

Mills took one last glance aft and dived down the hatch. Bell followed, grabbing the hatch lanyard as he slid down the ladder and pulled the hatch shut. Childress dogged it.

"One hundred feet," Bell shouted to the control room as his eyes went to the depth gauge. *Shark*, as usual, was hanging at thirty-six feet.

"Crazy fly-boys!" Mills spit, mentally bracing himself for the bombs that were sure to fall.

"All ahead emergency," Bell ordered. "Fifteen degree down bubble."

*Shark* broke the hang and slid under, picking up speed and angle of descent. They waited for the explosions, tensely watching the depth gauge. *Shark* leveled off at a hundred feet.

Childress was shaking and sweating. It was maddening standing there waiting for the end. He tightly clenched his trembling fingers. Damn it, he thought, he *had* to get a grip on himself. Didn't anyone but him ever feel fear?

Minutes passed, and no bombs fell. Mills was puzzled, then doubtful. "Who spotted that plane?" he asked.

"Willie the Silent," Jim Bell said.

Mills pursed his lips, nodding. "Then it must be so."

They waited another ten minutes at a hundred feet. Then Mills said, "Okay, Jim. Take her up and have a look around."

Bell ordered, "Periscope depth." That was sixty feet, the depth at which the periscope glass broke water. At sixty-five feet, Childress raised the periscope, and Bell knelt on the deck. When the fold-up T-bar handles came up out of the well, he grabbed them, unfolded them, put his eye into the rubber eyepiece, adjusted the power and focus in the handle, and "walked" the periscope around the horizon. He saw nothing but endless sea and sky.

"It's gone," he said.

They exhaled a collective sigh of relief. Childress stopped shaking and sweating. Next time, he said to himself, he *had to be calm*. Otherwise he'd be useless baggage, sure to be drummed out of submarines and sent to surface ship duty.

Mills said to Bell, "Surface and resume course."

And so it was done. Childress noted tersely in the logbook: "*1321. Dived from plane. 1345. Surfaced.*"

## CHAPTER TWELVE

At 1555, the four-to-eight watch relieved. Jack Childress and the rest of the bridge watch leisurely went below to the conning tower, then the control room, where the new watch was taking over. Childress much preferred to be topside, where the air was fresh and invigorating. Belowdecks, although the boat was spotlessly clean, the stench of diesel oil permeated everything. And he hated the belowdecks roll and pitch. It was difficult to get about or find a comfortable spot.

Childress walked aft to the crew's mess where most of the off-watch men were gathering. The two cooks—Freddie Lyman and his assistant, a baker, John Webster—were in the galley in whites and chefs' hats. They worked like slaves, putting out three meals a day for eighty-six men, plus baking bread, pies, cakes, and doughnuts and making sure the coffee urn and ice-cream machines were always full. They were a great pair, Childress thought. They even took time to make stacks of sandwiches for the men coming off watch. No men in the U.S. Navy were better fed than the crew of *Shark*. Mills insisted on that.

Childress passed up the sandwich stack. He prided himself on keeping lean and fit, and after only one war patrol, he was putting on weight. They all did. They had no means of working off calories.

He passed through the crowded, noisy mess and opened a door to the darkened crew's sleeping compartment. Here it was muted, quiet. And cold. The air-conditioning system was rigged to give a disproportionate outflow into this space because most men liked to sleep in a cold area, under blankets. There were a dozen off-watch men snoring away.

Childress made his way to his bunk at the bottom of the tier on the portside forward. A cozy spot. He knelt by his bunk and reached to dial the combination on his personal locker that was recessed in the bulkhead. Each crew member had one locker, and Childress's was about one cubic foot in size, just large enough to store two or three sets of dungarees, skivvies, white hat, socks, and regulation shoes, plus a toilet kit, two or three cartons of cigarettes, and a few personal items. Childress had left most of his gear stored on a tender in Midway. Someday he would get it back. Or that was the theory.

Childress opened the locker and took out a notebook and a thick mimeographed book entitled *Qualification Manual*, a highly technical book describing in dense text and diagrams every air and mechanical system on *Shark*. In order to "qualify" in submarines—and win the right to wear the coveted dolphin insignia on his lower right sleeve—Childress would have to learn every system on the boat. He would be required to copy the dozens of diagrams in his own notebook, and then he would have to pass a rigorous test. The Old Man's policy was that all men should qualify by the end of two patrols, and those who didn't were transferred off the boat. Because of the brevity of the last patrol, Childress still had much work to do.

He took his materials to the crew's mess, the only place on the boat where it was possible to study. By now, most of the off-watch men had had a snack and hit the sack. A few new men were studying at the tables, and there were a few old, qualified hands playing cribbage and acey-deucy, a form of backgammon. The boat's radio was turned to Tokyo Rose, who played the best and most contemporary music. No one paid any attention to her propaganda—until she mentioned a submarine by name.

He took a seat, turned his manual to a diagram of the boat's two-hundred-pound air system, and began carefully copying the diagram into his notebook. The system was not foreign to him because he had already diagramed it in sub school. He was hard at this work when a loud, throaty voice, unmistakably the Old Man, came on the PA system.

*"Attention all hands! Attention all hands!"* A sailor reached over and turned the volume down on Tokyo Rose.

*"This is the captain speaking. Our designated area for this patrol is Japanese Empire waters, in the vicinity of Tokyo Bay. We have been ordered to conduct a highly classified intelligence mission. A—uh—reconnaissance mission, the nature of which you will be apprised of as is necessary. I'm sorry to say we will not be attacking any ships this patrol. However, the special mission is an exacting one and of great importance. If suc-*

cessful, the submarine combat pin and other suitable awards will be authorized."

He paused a moment, then resumed. "Men, I'm proud to serve on board Shark with you. With your continued outstanding performance, and with the help of God, we shall succeed."

There was a moment's silence in the crew's mess as all hands contemplated the captain's message. Then, a cacophony of excited babble: wild speculation on the nature of the special mission.

Bob Pierpont entered the compartment from the control room and tacked a chart of the Pacific Ocean on the bulletin board. The ship's track, from Majuro to Tokyo Bay, was penciled in, with estimated positions along the track labeled Day 1, Day 2, etc. In all, it would be a 2,300-mile journey, seven days and seven nights at the customary two-engine long-distance cruising speed.

Wiping his hands on his apron, Freddie Lyman came from the galley and studied the chart. He said to Pierpont, "What's this special mission?"

Pierpont knew, but Mills had sworn him to secrecy. He shrugged and said, "I don't know," in a way that clearly indicated he did. He drew a cup of coffee, sat down beside Childress, and looked at the diagram Childress had drawn. "Not bad," he said.

"We had this at sub school," Childress said. "I should have kept my notebook."

"Here's a question they always ask," Pierpont said. "You're under attack. You dive. The diving officer says, 'Blow negative,' to stop the descent. The negative tank blow valve is frozen. You can't blow negative or main ballast or safety. How do you stop the descent?"

Childress pondered this for a long time. He had no idea.

"It's a trick question," said Pierpont. "Nobody ever gets it. Up in the control room, on the deck beneath the Christmas tree, there's a little bypass valve hardly anybody knows about. With this valve, you can tap into the two-hundred-pound air system and blow negative."

"No shit?"

"No shit," said Pierpont. "Check it out. Find the valve; because you're damned well going to get the question. But don't tell anyone I told you."

The air was suddenly shattered by the blood-curdling scream of the collision alarm. An urgent voice on the PA system announced: *"Collision in the maneuvering room! Collision in the maneuvering room! This is a drill. Repeat. This is a drill."*

Pierpont and five other men leaped up to rig the compartment for collision. One slammed shut and dogged the watertight door to the control room. Another closed the bulkhead flapper in the ventilation system. Freddie Lyman manned the sound-powered telephone. Childress sat rooted to his seat, his heart pounding wildly.

That was only the beginning. For the next five days, Mills ordered one drill after another. Fire. Chlorine gas in the forward battery. Chlorine gas in the after battery. Collision again. Fire again. Between disaster drills, they drilled at battle stations torpedo, conducted a simulated surface gun attack, and even held a man-overboard drill. There was not a minute's rest, nor would there be until they reached the patrol area. That was the Old Man's policy. Drill. Drill. Drill. To be a winner, you had to do the fundamentals automatically.

# CHAPTER THIRTEEN

After Martinez cleared away the dishes, the wardroom table, covered in green baize, became an office. Bill Hunt and Jim Bell laid out their work. Bell's off-watch duties were arduous. As communications officer, it was his responsibility to decode all SubPac radio dispatches addressed to *Shark*. Under ordinary circumstances, they could expect only four or five dispatches per patrol, but Mills had insisted that Bell decode every message addressed to all submarines on patrol. Bell could see no good reason for this, other than curiosity about what was going on in the sub force at sea.

Bell stacked the mountain of messages in chronological order, opened the code book, and set up the strip cipher. He was dead tired, and he could hardly keep his eyes open. Between watch standing, drills and decoding, he got only two or three hours sleep out of every twenty-four, and he was falling farther and farther behind in the decoding.

Bill Hunt did not stand watches. His primary operating responsibility was navigation of the ship: plotting the course, taking sun lines and star sights a few times a day. This was not a taxing load, especially since Bob Pierpont, assistant navigator as well as head of the quartermasters and signalmen, was a superb navigator. Pierpont was the best quartermaster Hunt had ever seen, so that part of Hunt's job was easy— and fun.

But Hunt's administrative duties were staggering. He was, in effect, the chief administrative officer on the boat. Every buck stopped on his desk. Food. Personnel. Mechanical. The upward flow of paper work, both important and trivial, was awesome.

Hunt loved every minute of it. He was absolutely delighted to have been sprung from the Sub-Pac staff, to again have a deck under his feet, to be a key man among this superbly trained, thoroughly professional crew. His skills and discipline had come back to him at once. He had forgotten nothing about submarines; he was good at his job, meeting the high standards on *Shark*; and he was determined to set even higher standards of his own.

He paused to take a hard look at Bell, who had dozed off. He liked Bell. He was solid, methodical.

"Jim—" said Hunt.

Bell's eyes popped open.

"Knock it off and get some sleep," Hunt said. "Hit the sack. You're excused from all drills."

Bell pointed to the pile of dispatches. "They're getting ahead of me."

"Never mind," said Hunt. "You can't stand a proper deck watch in the shape you're in. I'll speak to the captain about all that decoding. Now this is an order. Hit the sack." He grinned.

Bell returned the grin. He had been no more impressed with Hunt on first meeting than the captain had been, but with the passing of each day, he saw new depths and strengths. Hunt was an insightful man. Bell rose gratefully and went off to bed.

Hunt returned to his mountain of paperwork, quickly going through a stack of official mail that had been picked up in Majuro. These were mostly routine, low-classified, nonpriority ALNAVs and technical letters and bulletins from Washington —the Secretary of the Navy, the Chief of Naval

Operations, the Bureau of Personnel, the Bureau of Ships, the Bureau of Ordnance. But each had to be acknowledged.

He scanned a "Restricted" directive from the Bureau of Personnel (Bu Pers). Halfway through, he stopped with an inward gasp and began to reread, very carefully, from the top.

To:  All Fleet Submarines
FROM:  The Bureau of Personnel
SUBJECT:  Personnel, Rotation of

1. Subject immediately, all personnel, officers and enlisted alike, shall be transferred to shore billets, new construction, or relief crews upon completion of five war patrols or fifteen months uninterrupted service, whichever is greater.

2. This policy has been arrived at only after prolonged study of human factors by an eminent panel of the nation's most highly qualified psychiatrists and psychologists. The panel's conclusion was that after the stated period of service in combat, a dangerous fatigue, which may not even be apparent, sets in, with resultant danger to the ship and to all hands. The fatigue is particularly pronounced in the cases of commanding officers who bear an unusual load of responsibility on war patrol.

3. There shall be no exceptions to this policy.

                    Louis E. Denfeld, Vice Admiral
                    Acting Chief, Bureau of Personnel

Hunt stared at the directive in amazement. He'd known something like this was in the works because he'd met some of the members of the panel when they visited SubPac staff for interviews, but he had no idea the policy was that close to being promulgated. And, he thought, what an oddly routine way to explode such a powerful bomb. The policy would decimate the crews of every boat in the sub force. Dozens of hotshot skippers with long combat experience would have to be relieved. Including John R. Mills.

Hunt walked aft to Mills's curtain door and rapped on the bulkhead.

"Come in." Mills boomed.

Walking on eggshells, Hunt opened the curtain. Mills was lying in his bunk, bare chested, reading *Untamed Ecstasy*, a battered paperback from the boat's one-shelf library. He sat up, throwing the book aside, muttering, "Trash."

"Sorry to disturb you, captain," Hunt said quietly, "but I thought you ought to see this Bu-Pers directive right away."

He handed the memo to Mills, who read it quickly and then read it again.

"This is crazy," muttered Mills, his eyes glued to the paper as though it were a cobra poised to strike. "They can't do this. It'll destroy the sub force! What's the matter with those idiots in Washington? Don't they know there's a war on, for Christ's sake? Combat fatigue! What a lot of bullshit! I talked to those fucking shrinks in Midway. They're all a bunch of assholes."

He broke off, suddenly silent.

Hunt had never seen a man so crushed, so utterly despairing. "I'm sure they'll give you new construction, captain. A brand-new boat, a new crew."

Mills wasn't listening. "That means me, Pops, Pierpont, Nutting, Gilsey, Webb, Nelson, Barr . . ." He couldn't go on with the list. It was like a litany of the dead.

Hunt silently backed out of the cabin and returned to his work in the wardroom regretting that he had so precipitously confronted Mills with the directive, that he had been the king's messenger bearing such grim news. But that was his job. No purpose would have been served by postponing the news.

The character of the submarine war against Japan was changing. He had seen that in his six months on the SubPac staff. Where once the sub force had been dominated by a handful of flamboyant and recklessly heroic men—Fearless Freddie Warder, Mush Morton, Sam Dealey, Creed Cardwell Burlingame, Mauler Mills—the emphasis was now turning to scientific methodology. The bureaucrats and statisticians were ascendant, and the BuPers directive was symbolic of the new approach.

Still troubled, Hunt retackled his paperwork, but he was unable for the moment to concentrate. There was a good possibility that Mills might not snap back with the famous old resilience and indomitability. He might lapse into a dangerous depression, go off the deep end, do something desperate, and that, in turn, might place a heavy responsibility on Hunt, make his job as exec infinitely more ticklish and difficult than it already was. Mills might even vent his anger and frustration on him, for if ever there was a symbol of the new methodology, it was Bill Hunt.

# CHAPTER FOURTEEN

Freddie Lyman was inordinately sensitive and conscientious. He watched the crew at mealtimes like a hen clucking over her brood. He knew the chowhounds and the picky eaters, and he was sensitive to signs of displeasure or changes in eating habits. After the third dinner sitting, he approached the radar technician, Al Weir, a noted glutton. "What's wrong, Al? You didn't eat a thing," said Lyman.

"Not hungry," said Weir.

"You didn't like the veal?"

"Will you get off my back?" Weir snapped. "I don't have to apologize for not eating your chow."

Weir walked on to the dimmed-out control room, then to the forward battery, where he found Jim Bell in his stateroom. "You wanted to see me?" Weir asked.

Bell had sent for Weir some four hours earlier, but Weir never came when sent for. It was a game he played. Usually Bell was forced to seek him out. Now Bell was furious, but he gave no sign of it.

"Here's a directive from BuShips on the SJ radar," Bell said, handing Weir a two-page single-spaced document bucked down from Hunt.

Weir sat on Bell's bunk to read, further angering Bell. There was nothing written in regulations, but an enlisted man did not sit on an officer's bunk unless invited.

Weir returned the document with a sneer. "This is all bullshit."

"Bullshit?" said Bell, taken aback. The document directed that all vessels modify the SJ radar with a Mark 5, Mod 8 power booster.

"Yeah," Weir went on. "I was part of the team that experimented with that booster at the radar lab in Anacostia. It was a complete flop."

"But it says it will increase the range by six to eight thousand yards."

"I'm telling you it's a flop," Weir said. "I . . ." He felt a sharp pain in his upper stomach, a fleeting wave of nausea.

"What's the matter?" said Bell. "Are you all right?"

"I don't know," Weir said. "I feel strange."

"See the Doc," said Bell. "We can't afford to have you under the weather."

Weir returned to the subject. "I can't believe they put through that change order. In our experiment, the booster continually blew out the primary cathode tube."

"Perhaps they perfected it after you left," Bell suggested.

"No. They couldn't have. There are certain physical laws that can't be altered or circumvented. You'll have to take my word for it. BuShips is full of shit. I'm sure some electrical company bribed a project officer to approve this."

Bell was shocked and irritated, but he lacked the technical expertise in electronics to argue with Weir.

Weir felt oddly light-headed and nauseous again. As far as he was concerned, the booster issue was closed, and without another word he stood up and walked out, going to the forward torpedo room for the evening movie, a scratchy print of a Mickey Rooney turkey, *Girl Crazy*. Weir sat through the crew's jeering and hissing for five minutes, then left.

He walked aft. The pain in his upper stomach struck again, this time so sharply he gasped. Was it a heart attack? No, he thought, too low for that.

He found Doc Jones playing cribbage in the crew's mess. The shipboard cribbage tournament had been organized and launched, and Doc was in charge. If past history meant anything, he was the odds-on favorite to take the three-hundred-dollar winner's purse. His only real competition would be the Old Man.

Weir sat down and waited until Doc pegged out to win. Then he said, "Can I see you a minute?"

Doc Jones sighed and got up. What now? he wondered. Weir always had something. Usually imaginary.

They found a little privacy in the passageway.

"I've got a hell of a pain right here," Weir said, pressing his upper stomach. "I think it might be my appendix."

"Have you taken a shit lately?" Doc asked. Constipation was common after four weeks on the beach.

"Well, I've not been regular," Weir conceded. "What are the symptoms of appendicitis?"

"Loss of appetite, nausea, pain in the upper stomach," Doc said. "You don't have appendicitis, for Christ's sake. It could be a hundred other things."

"I've got all those symptoms," Weir insisted.

"We'll see about that," Doc said. "Just wait a few days and see if nature takes its course."

Weir, suddenly enraged at Doc's monumental indifference, barked, "I'm sick, you damned quack!"

"Well, if you have appendicitis, I can't give you anything anyway," Doc said, fighting his own anger. "Come see me after you move your bowels."

Weir stalked off. Doc watched him go, concluding once again that Weir was not temperamentally qualified for submarine duty. Far from it. He was a pain in the ass. There were so few of these radar technicians that SubPac had been forced to waive the usual psychological screening process, and *Shark* had been unlucky enough to draw a prima donna—and a hypochondriac to boot!

Red Weaver, the boat's yeoman, reputed to be the fastest typist in the sub force, tacked the personnel list—together with a copy of the Bu-Pers directive—on the bulletin board in the crew's mess. No one bothered to consult the documents. The word had long since spread. Everyone knew which three of the eight officers and which twenty of the seventy-eight enlisted men would be leaving the boat after this patrol.

Bob Pierpont was still outraged. He could talk of nothing else. He found Pops Wheeler smoking his after-chow cigar in the chief's quarters. Wheeler read the document Pierpont shoved into his hand: a request for a waiver.

"No use my putting this through, Bob," Pops said wearily. "The exec'll just buck it back down. The directive is clear on that. Quote, there shall be no exceptions, unquote. Why don't you cool down? We could all use a blow on the beach—especially the Old Man."

"What'd you mean by *that?*"

"You're not objective enough when it comes to the captain, Bob. Look at his face real close. The eyes—hell, he's tired."

"What are you doing?" demanded Pierpont. "Sucking up to BuPers? You bucking for warrant?"

"Blow it out your ass," Wheeler snapped.

"You agree with the policy?" Pierpont insisted.

"Yes, goddamn it, I agree," Wheeler conceded. "In my own case, anyway. I need to get home. Something's wrong with Sally."

Pierpont was suddenly solicitous. They were old friends. "What's the trouble, Pops?"

"I'm not sure, but the last couple of letters have sounded funny. And I got a letter from Susie, our oldest daughter, and she says she thinks her mother is sick. I've just got to get home soon. I'm worried half to death."

"Jeez, Pops, that's too bad. I'm really sorry to hear it."

They fell silent. After a time, Pierpont returned to the BuPers policy, but he was more subdued. "This is going to kill the Old Man, not cure him."

"They'll give him new construction, for sure."

"But that's a pain in the ass," said Pierpont. "At least nine months on the beach, hassling with BuShips reps in the shipyard, tons of paperwork and thousands of meetings. You know what it's like. You've been through it. The Old Man ain't cut out for that crap. He'll wind up in hack or be sent to Siberia."

"Not with those four Navy Crosses," Wheeler said. "That carries a hell of a lot of weight these days. No pip-squeak BuShips rep is going to take on Mauler Mills. They'll give him everything he wants, and then some."

"No," insisted Pierpont. "Deep down he's vulnerable. Too nice a guy."

"Maybe he'll settle down and get married. Raise a family."

"Oh bullshit, Pops. You're always trying to get everybody married off."

They heard a sharp rapping on the captain's bulkhead across the passageway. It was the watch messenger from the control room saying excitedly, "Report from the officer of the deck, sir. Radar contact, two-five-zero, range fifteen thousand yards."

Pierpont felt his blood surge as he dashed from the chief's quarters to the control room. They were deep in Japanese waters, closing the coast of Honshu, near Hachijo Jima, in the Nampo Shoto. It could only be the enemy.

# CHAPTER FIFTEEN

Bill Hunt was sound asleep, pleasantly dreaming about Sharon, his fiancée. The PA speaker over his bunk jarred him awake: *"Station the tracking party! Station the tracking party!"* and he piled groggily out of his bunk, reaching for his shoes.

Jim Bell, with whom he shared the compartment, sat up in the dark. "What is it?"

"I don't know," Hunt said, putting on his shirt. "Another drill, I guess."

Bell groaned, lay down, rolled over, and was instantly asleep again.

Hunt put on a pair of red night-adaptation goggles and stepped into the passageway. There was something electric in the air, and his instinct told him it was more than a drill. He hurried to the dimmed-out control room. Red Weaver had already set up the plotting table, assisted by Tony Walker and by Quartermaster Childress, whom Pierpont had recommended for a tryout, replacing Signalman Carl Corley on the tracking team. Pierpont had told Hunt that Corley had requested relief from the party, but had given no reasons.

"Have Martinez send up two cups of coffee." It was Mills, booming down from the bridge. He sounded in fine fettle. The watch messenger hurried to the wardroom.

Hunt removed his goggles and took his place on a stool in front of the plotting table. "What the hell's going on?" he said to Weaver.

"Convoy," said Weaver, busily working with dividers, protractor, and parallel rule, plotting in data from radar. He was good at this, a real pro. So was the gunner's mate, Walker, another old hand. Childress was getting the knack.

Hunt had to admire Jack Mills. He never let an opportunity go by to drill the crew. But this was one for the books: deep in Japanese waters, drilling on a *real* convoy. You couldn't ask for a more realistic experience. And drill it had to be. The operational order from Voge had been specific: *Shark* would not—repeat not—engage in action with enemy vessels except in self-defense.

"Range one-one-oh-oh-oh," Al Weir on radar reported. Hunt wondered how Weir was feeling tonight and whether the complaint Doc had noted on the daily medical report had cleared up.

"Bearing zero-nine-four," a voice intoned. It was Bob Pierpont on the bridge.

What was Pierpont doing on the bridge? Hunt wondered. *Shark* was not at battle stations; they were merely drilling the tracking party. It seemed that little occurred on *Shark* beyond Pierpont's ken. He was like a surrogate chief of the boat and skipper rolled into one. The Old Man's alter ego, Hunt thought. If they were not being transferred off, it could become a real problem. He wondered how Mike Reynolds had dealt with it.

Martinez came from the wardroom with two mugs of steaming coffee and went up the conning-tower ladder with great agility, one mug in each hand. Hunt wondered who the other mug was meant for. The answer came in an angry flash: Pierpont. So the wardroom mess steward was now waiting on Pierpont, too. That could not sit well with the rest of the crew.

The tracking party solved the convoy course and speed quickly and passed it up to the conning tower and bridge. Down came a comment from Mills, who never failed to give credit where it was due: "Good work, tracking team."

On the bridge, Mills was glued to the TBT; his steaming coffee mug was unattended on the fairwater. Sipping the hot liquid, Pierpont stood behind Mills wondering what was going through the Old Man's head. He had seldom seen him so alert and coolly professional. If this was merely a drill, he was putting on a damned good show.

"Captain," reported Al Weir, "I now count twenty-eight ships. Four columns of five, plus eight escorts. One in the van, three on each flank, and a trailer astern."

Jesus! Pierpont thought. What a target!

"Very well, Al," Mills responded, suppressing his excitement. Never had he encountered so large a convoy. "I've got them all in sight now— Range?"

"Nine-five-oh-oh," Weir said. Four and a half nautical miles.

Instinctively Mills turned and looked at the moon. It was a half-moon, directly overhead, obscured from time to time by dark scudding clouds. Perfect. In his mind, he set up the approach, laying out a mental track so that he fired parallel to the trough between seas, where the torpedoes would run most smoothly.

"Have a look," Mills said to Pierpont, stepping back from the TBT. Pierpont had binoculars, but the TBT was a more stable platform.

Pierpont slowly swept the convoy, his heart surging. Jesus H. Christ! Big, big tankers. Big *new* tankers. Each one loaded to the gunnels! Millions of barrels of fuel oil from Borneo or Java, almost home now.

"Keerist!" said Pierpont, stepping back from the TBT.

"How the convoy slipped by the code breakers, I'll never know," said Mills. It was against regulations for a skipper to even discuss the Japanese code breakers with anyone, let alone with an enlisted man, but there were no secrets between Mills and Pierpont.

"Somebody dropped the ball," Pierpont said, using the Old Man's favorite metaphor for error. "For sure nobody's laid a glove on that convoy."

Mills turned suddenly to Pierpont. "What do you think?"

"You *know* what I think, captain," Pierpont said.

Mills spoke into the intercom: "Ask Mr. Hunt to come to the bridge, please."

Hunt was on the bridge in less than a minute, and Mills said to him, "Take a look at that. A submarine skipper's dream!"

Hunt put his eyes into the TBT binoculars and swept the convoy. His heart went to his throat. Ship after ship after ship. Magnified seven times, they seemed close enough to touch. This was the first time Hunt had seen the enemy. It was unreal, like a film.

"There must be twenty million barrels of oil in those tankers," said Mills. "Enough to keep the emperor's aircraft and ships going for a month."

They knew a good deal about Japan's oil shortage from the U.S. Navy's code breakers. Nowadays, after aircraft carriers, tankers were the highest priority targets for the sub force. Stop the flow of oil, the statisticians had pronounced, and the Japanese war machine would cease to function.

"That convoy hasn't been touched," Mills went on. "It's about to put six points on the board." He paused. "What do you think, Mr. Hunt?"

Hunt knew exactly what the question meant. *Shark*'s orders were specific, but this convoy was of immense strategic value to the Japanese. The code breakers had somehow failed to learn of its sailing, a rare lapse. Now, it was almost home free. Only *Shark* stood between the convoy and safety. Should they disobey the orders and attack?

Hunt weighed the question. Then he said, "No. It's not our responsibility, captain."

"The *war*'s our responsibility," Mills returned, his anger rising.

"You're not going to win it tonight," Hunt said. "Single-handedly."

Mills narrowed his eyes in rage, staring at his exec. Hunt was a good man with paperwork, the best Mills had ever seen. Give him 4.0 on that. But did he have courage? Was he hiding behind that paper?

"You sound just like the admiral! What's the matter with that goddamned SubPac staff? Don't they know the job of submariners is to sink ships? Not run around on Hollywood reconnaissance errands inside Tokyo Bay?" This allusion was to the Cary Grant melodrama, *Des-*

*tination Tokyo,* a new film the crew had seen—
and hooted—in Majuro. "The crew's had it up to
here with this stupid mission. Right, Pierpont?"

"Yes, sir, captain," Pierpont said a little too
eagerly.

Hunt saw that he was again walking on eggshells. One thing had remained unspoken: it
would be the last time in a long time, perhaps the
last time ever, that Mauler Mills would have an
opportunity to sink enemy ships.

"We could fudge the patrol report," said Mills.
"Say we were surprised, that we were attacked
and counterattacked in self-defense."

"You wouldn't get away with it," said Hunt.

"I should never have accepted those stupid orders!" Mills shouted.

Hunt remained silent, staring at Mills, who
ranted on.

"There's never been a better setup! We've got
a full load of fish. Perfect moon and sea. Good
position on the convoy. They're so close to home,
they're probably relaxed and overconfident, dop-
ing off. We—"

"Range six-five-oh-oh," Weir reported crisp-
ly.

"Very well," Mills said distantly. He turned to
Hunt. "You know, it's probably the last shot at
the enemy a lot of us will have."

"Yes," Hunt said. "I realize that."

"That oil will kill a lot of GIs."

"Yes," Hunt said, determined to remain neutral.

"What happened to the old SubPac bird-in-
hand policy?" Mills said, groping. "Shoot first,
worry about it later?"

"I don't know, captain," said Hunt. "Things are
changing."

"Well, shit!" said Mills, slamming his fist on the
fairwater. As he paced the narrow bridge, Hunt
and Pierpont squeezed aside to give him space.
Hunt could see that the big Hamlet scene was
drawing to a close. Naval discipline was too deep-

ly ingrained. Mills could not bring himself to disobey a direct written order.

"What if our mission fails?" he said to Hunt in a final sputter. "Then we've thrown this convoy away for nothing."

"We won't fail, captain," Hunt said.

"Well, shit," Mills muttered again into the wind, and grunting and mumbling to himself, he examined the convoy once more through the TBT.

After a moment, he backed away, closed the lens caps, and said quietly into the intercom, "Secure the tracking party. Secure the tracking party."

Al Weir came on the intercom. "Did we hear you right on that, captain? Secure the tracking party?"

"Yes!" Mills erupted in rage. "Are you deaf? Secure the goddamned tracking party!"

"Secure the tracking party, aye," Weir said, this time without a trace of irony.

To avoid any awkward epilogues, Pierpont went below, thinking the Old Man would want to be alone. There was a sense of anticlimax in the control room. Red Weaver, Tony Walker, and Jack Childress were packing away the plotting gear. Trying to head off the inevitable grilling, Pierpont said to Weaver, "How'd my boy do tonight?" He meant Childress.

"Real good," said Weaver, the most senior of the tracking party, an old hand.

"Pierpont-trained," Pierpont said with exaggerated pride.

"But what's the poop?" said Weaver, his voice low, forcing the main point. "How come we let them go?"

"Orders."

"Orders?" Weaver said. "What kind of war patrol is this?"

"You'll see, Red," said Pierpont with his superior, mysterious air.

"I bet it hurt the Old Man," said Weaver.

"You bet it did," said Pierpont.

"My old adrenaline was flowing," said Weaver.

"Mine, too," said Pierpont.

"But now I'm just as glad," said Weaver.

Pierpont knew what that meant. Red Weaver had developed a fixation that he wouldn't get out of the war alive—that somewhere out there was a Jap bullet with his name on it. Pierpont had urged the Old Man to beach Weaver two patrols back, but the Old Man had said no. Weaver had been with him a long time, and the Old Man was loath to break up the old gang. "When you're on a winning streak, you don't change your backfield or playbook," was the way he had put it.

## CHAPTER SIXTEEN

Steering a near due west course, *Shark* approached the Nampo Shoto from the east. It was night; the boat remained on the surface. In the conning tower, Hunt and Pierpont bent over a chart on the desk. Pierpont had plotted the series of star sights they had taken after sunset, and according to their exacting calculations, within the hour *Shark* should make a landfall on Mikura Jima, a small volcanic island about eighty miles due south of Tokyo Bay. After a voyage of 2,300 miles a landfall was still a ticklish business, wide open for error, and in these island-pocked enemy waters there was no room for error. Torn by doubt, Hunt fretted over their calculations.

At 2210, Al Weir, manning the radar for this special occasion, reported, "Radar contact on land: bearing three-oh-oh, range twenty-five miles."

Using dividers and parallel rulers, Pierpont plotted the contact. "That's it!" he cried. Mikura Jima was only eight miles in diameter, but the rocky volcano jutted to three thousand feet, and that was what Weir's radar beams had bounced off at such long range.

Hunt was immensely pleased. He had not made a landfall since he served on *Pickerel* in 1940, and then it had only been an exercise. He had not been the navigator. He had retained more of the science than he would have thought possible; nonetheless, it was comforting to have had Pierpont as an assistant.

Hunt passed word to the control room. "Tell the captain we made landfall on Mikura Jima at 2210, radar range fifty thousand yards."

"Aye," said the watch messenger. He returned a moment later to report, "Captain gives his compliments to Mr. Hunt and Quartermaster Pierpont."

Pierpont unfolded a piece of paper with a list of the crew. Behind each name there was a time noted. This was the landfall pool. All hands had contributed one dollar each, and the man who guessed the time closest to 2210 would win the pot—eighty-six dollars. Running his finger down the list, Pierpont saw that it was Webster, John B., ship's baker second class, who had picked 2214.

Pierpont passed word to the control room: "The winner of the landfall pool is Johnny Webster, with 2214. Please post it on the bulletin board, along with the official time: 2210."

Pierpont was pleased. Johnny Webster was the most universally loved sailor on the boat. To celebrate his victory, he was sure to bake a pineapple upside-down cake, everybody's favorite, thus, all hands would benefit from his win.

The OOD, Wally Yates, spoke on the intercom. "All ahead one-third. Tell the captain we've entered dense fog."

Pierpont said to Hunt, "Kuroshio—the Japan Current." Hunt knew the waters well. The current was icy cold, and at this time of year dense fog was commonplace. A mixed blessing. It would shield them, but they would have to depend heavily on radar for navigating.

Mills came up to the conning tower and leaned over the radarscope. The green light reflected on his face. He said to Weir, "How's your calibration?"

"On the button," Weir said, seeming offended that anyone should even ask.

"Let's check it," said Mills. "It's been a long trip. We've got to be absolutely sure it's exactly on the button." He went to the intercom. "Wally, we're going to check out the SJ. I'll take the conn for a while and put her midway between Mikura Jima and Inamba Jima."

"Aye, aye, captain," said Wally Yates. "Visibility up here is nil, sir."

Inamba Jima was a small uninhabited rock pinnacle twenty miles southwest of Mikura Jima. Both were precisely plotted on the charts, and by placing *Shark* midway between them, Mills could check the known ranges and thus determine whether the radar was in calibration.

*Shark* reached position within thirty minutes, and the radar calibrated exactly, giving strong pips on both islands at range twenty thousand yards.

"Okay," Mills said to Weir, satisfied with the check-out. "Baby that thing like it was your own child. Believe me, our whole mission—and the lives of the men—will depend on how well that machine performs."

Weir was miffed that the captain could think his machine anything less than perfect. "What is this damned mission?" he asked.

"We're going into Tokyo Bay," said Mills, turning abruptly and climbing the ladder to the bridge.

Weir sat staring at the radar in a state of shock. His eyes bulged, and he felt the sharp pain in his upper stomach. He turned to Hunt with an anxious look. "Tokyo Bay? What for?"

"Reconnaissance," Hunt said, on his way to go get a cup of coffee.

Hunt found Jim Bell in the wardroom deciphering a radio message for all submarines. Bell passed the message to Hunt. It was from SubPac.

*Fleet oiler Osage sunk in protected Eniwetok anchorage. Circumstances similar U.S.S. Florida. No known cause. Strong probability Japs have new secret naval weapon. Utmost concern on highest levels. All submarines exercise extreme caution. Break radio silence and report any unusual enemy activity that could shed light.*

Hunt reread the message. One battleship, and one fleet tanker sunk at anchor, far behind the front lines. And in each case, *inside* submarine nets. How was this possible? What the hell could it be? He finished his coffee and returned to the conning tower.

They eased toward the northwest at one-third speed in the dense fog. The bridge was depending entirely on the radar. Hunt and Pierpont, assisted by Childress, plotted their course and recommended changes, and Weir read off the ranges and bearings to the islands. They left Mikura Jima on the starboard hand and, for a time, had Miyake Jima, a large island, on the starboard beam and Zeni Su, a pinnacle, on the port beam. O Shima, a large island at the foot of Sagami Wan—the so-called outer Tokyo Bay—lay thirty miles to the north, and the city of Tokyo itself lay only fifty-five miles beyond O Shima.

Mills peered into the gloom. It was hopeless. He could see nothing. But he could smell Japan.

An unusual northwesterly offshore breeze brought the odors.

"Smell that, Wally?" he said to the OOD. "That's Japan. Human shit, that's what it is. Fertilizer. Those yellow bellies don't waste anything." He stopped, listening intently. "What was that?"

"I heard it," Yates replied softly. "I don't know."

"All stop," Mills said into the intercom, his voice almost a whisper. They glided along in the fog in silence.

"It's laughter," Yates said, peering into the gloom.

"Yes," said Mills. "What the hell?"

At that instant, *Shark*'s sharp bow crashed into an object, and the ship shuddered and stopped. From the bow area, Mills and Yates could hear excited Japanese voices.

"We've hit a goddamned sampan!" Mills said to Yates. Then to the intercom, "All back emergency! Away the boarding party."

# CHAPTER SEVENTEEN

In the view of many, Tony Walker was an unlikely type for a gunner's mate. Most gunner's mates were big and dumb, like bos'ns. They were usually forced into the rating because they couldn't qualify for schools in other ratings. Walker hardly fitted the mold. He was short, pale and thin, and sharp as a tack. He had chosen gunnery because he had always been a gun nut, and it was his sharpness that had earned him a place with the tracking party.

Walker was sitting in the mess hall playing cribbage with Frank Nalle when *Shark* shuddered and stopped. He thought they had gone aground, but a second later word burst over the PA system: *"Away the boarding party! Away the boarding party!"*

"God Almighty!" shouted Walker, jumping up and throwing down a hand that was worth at least fifteen points. Walker, who was head of the six-man boarding party, was taken utterly by surprise. In his five war patrols, the boarding party had never been called away, except in drills. What the hell could that shudder be?

He opened the trapdoor to the ammo locker in the crew's mess. By that time, the other five members of the boarding party had run up in a state of excitement. These men had been picked for their size, their brawn, and their reputed toughness: Torpedoman Nutting; Machinist's Mates Nelson and Titus; Seamen Vogel and Neal. Each was six feet or more—and mean.

Walker quickly passed gear up from the locker: .45 pistols, knives, five Thompson submachine guns with ammo packs, a big steel crowbar, plastic explosives and fuses, and combat helmets camouflaged like those of the Marine Corps. He climbed out, wearing a .45 and carrying a twelve-gauge double-barreled shotgun. The men put on the gear and raced to the bridge.

"Boarding party reporting," Walker said to Mills as his men crowded onto the bridge. Seaman Neal carried the crowbar. Vogel carried the explosives.

"Shhhh," said Mills, a finger to his lips. All fell silent. They could hear the excited babble of Japanese voices, but because of the fog they could see nothing.

"All stop," Mills whispered into the intercom. Then to Walker, "We hit a sampan, I think. The damned thing's hooked onto us. Get down on deck and find out. If we're fouled, board and demolish her."

"Aye, aye," said Walker.

Mills watched the men climb down on deck. Luckily, the seas were dead calm. There was no roll, no pitch, no danger of a man falling over the side. He spoke to the conning tower: "Boarding party on deck. Keep a sharp watch on radar." It would not do to be surprised by an enemy destroyer or a patrol boat.

Tony Walker led his team down on the wet wood-slat deck. He moved into the fog, slowly and tensely, a finger on one trigger of his shotgun, and when he turned to look back he could no longer see the bridge or even the line of men he was leading.

Directly in his path, a face appeared out of the fog. Walker would never forget it. It was a small old Oriental face with leathery, wrinkled skin, squinty eyes, and wispy white hair. Walker froze and fired in one motion, and one barrel of the shotgun exploded with hideous flame and force. The Oriental face disappeared.

Walker squatted and waved his arm, calling the party forward. They deployed across the width of the boat, their Thompsons aimed into the foggy nothingness.

When Walker shouted, "Fire!" the five men opened up. Even above the noise, they could hear the screams and moans, and when Walker raised his arm and the men stopped firing, there was no longer the slightest sound. Whoever had climbed on the deck of *Shark* was now dead.

The party moved forward on the narrowing deck, passing the T-shaped JP sonar head, the capstan, and the chocks and bitts. They came up against a jagged wooden barricade: the broadside of a big sampan, wedged firmly on *Shark's* bow!

Walker couldn't believe his eyes. "From **a**

skirmish line," he whispered to his men. "Shoot anything that moves. I'll report to the captain."

He slowly retraced his steps along the deck and climbed up on the bridge. "We've hit a sampan, all right, captain," he said. "Boarders repelled, skirmish line in place. But, sir, we're stuck in her side, tight as a big pecker in a knothole."

Mills burst into laughter. He turned to Pierpont, who had come to the bridge with Hunt. "Be sure you log those exact words," he said. "By God, Walker, you'll make military history with that quote."

"Sorry, sir," Walker said. He was a shy Alabamian with no ambition to make history.

"Can you blow her away?" Mills asked.

"Don't think so, sir," said Walker. "We might damage our bow."

"Mmmmmmmm," said Mills.

Hunt was astonished by the captain's coolness and apparent lack of concern. They were in one damned mess.

"Can you burn her away?" Mills asked.

"Yes, sir," said Walker. "Be a hell of a fire, sir. If the fog lifts . . ."

"Burn her away," said Mills.

Walker went below and soon returned with a five-gallon can of gasoline. He went forward to his men and laid out the plan. Feeling their way in the fog amidst a shambles of lines, fishnet, and sails, they climbed onto the deck of the sampan. Walker heard a rustling noise, a grunt, then a splash. It was another Jap going over the side.

Walker spewed the gasoline along the deck, torched it with his Zippo lighter, and it burst into flame. "Okay! Get off! Back on the boat!" he shouted.

He turned to retrace his steps, then paused, listening. His heart dropped. He could hear a baby crying somewhere below. Without thinking twice, he plunged into the foul-smelling cabin, and there he found the baby, tightly bound in cloth, lying on a straw mat. He scooped it up and raced back up the steps to the deck. The boat was in flames.

Walker tossed his shotgun over the side, held the baby tightly in his arms, and jumped. The icy water closed over his head, and he fought to the surface, sputtering, swimming with one arm, holding the screaming baby out of the water with the other.

Torpedoman Nutting was first to reach Shark's bridge. By then the sampan was a roaring mass, a big eerie red glow in the fog. After Nutting, came Neal, Vogel, Titus, and Nelson.

"Where the hell's Walker?" Mills demanded.

"He was aft on the poop," said Nutting. "He set the fire."

"He yelled for us to get off," said Vogel, "but I didn't see him after that."

Mills felt a chill in his chest. He said to Nutting, "Take two men; search the forward deck." But he knew that was futile. He had to believe that Walker was gone. He turned, tears filming his eyes, and silently faced the great flaming pyre on Shark's bow.

Still holding the baby out of the water, Walker kept close to the bulbous barnacle-encrusted saddle tanks on Shark's hull. He stopped and looked up. He could scarcely see four feet in the fog, not even to the limber holes above the saddle tanks, and he could only guess where he might be. His great concern was sharks. He had never seen a shark, but he was terrified of them.

He lay on his back in the water, cupped his free hand to his mouth, and shouted, "Bridge! Captain!"

The lookout, Harry Barr, standing high in the shears, heard Walker's voice faintly above the roar of the flames. He listened until he was certain, then he shouted to Mills, whom he couldn't see in the fog, "Captain! There's a man calling you. He's in the water on the starboard side. It must be Tony."

"What?" said Mills. "Where?"

"Starboard side," Barr shouted.

Mills turned to Vogel and Neal. "Get him aboard! Hurry!"

Vogel and Neal jumped on deck and ran to the starboard side, shouting into the fog, "Tony! Tony!"

"Here! Here, you assholes!"

Neal, vectoring on the sound of Tony's voice, climbed down on the rounded saddle tank. He held onto a rusty, jagged limber hole. Now he could see Walker, blessedly alive.

"Take this baby," said Walker, holding up what seemed to be a bundle of rags.

"What?" said Neal, stupefied.

"Baby!" said Walker. "Don't drop it."

Neal grabbed the baby and handed it up to Vogel. "That's a *baby* in there," he said, still disbelieving.

Walker, relieved of his burden, grabbed Neal's extended hand and pulled himself up on the saddle tank. "Had to fucking jump," he gasped. "Lost my shotgun."

Walker took the baby, and the three men went up to the bridge. Walker handed the baby to Mills, said, "One prisoner, sir," and the baby again burst into cries of anguish.

Mills, cradling the baby in his arms, pulled the cloth aside and tickled its chubby cheek with his huge forefinger. "There, there," he said softly as he rocked it in his huge teddy-bear arms. But still it cried.

"Take it below," Mills said, suddenly turning to Pierpont. "Have Doc look her—or him—over for communicable diseases. Give it shots, if necessary. And something to eat."

"Aye, aye, sir," said Pierpont, accepting the screaming bundle. "I'll have to log him—her—it—in. What shall we call it?"

Mills replied, "Lockwood-san."

The fire suddenly died. They could only see a dull red glow in the fog. Walker went forward for an inspection and came back to report the sampan burned out, completely gutted. "If we dive," he said, "I think the rest of it will come off and pop to the surface, captain."

"Good idea," said Mills. He turned and shouted, "Clear the decks! Clear the bridge!"

There was the usual mad dash for the hatch, but Mills did not crash-dive. Alone on the bridge, he said to the intercom, "Are all hands present and accounted for?"

"Wait, captain," a voice said. Presently the same voice said, "Officer of the deck reports all hands who were on deck, including the watch and boarding party, accounted for."

"Very well," Mills said. "Wally, I want a slow stationary dive."

"Aye, aye, sir," Yates replied. "We're all prepared for that."

Good, Mills thought; they were anticipating him again. "Okay," he said. "Pull the cork."

Mills descended the ladder to the conning tower, closing the hatch by the lanyard, and the quartermaster of the watch dogged it. Yates took her down horizontally, very slowly, to fifty feet. Through the hull, they could hear the spit and hiss as the hot timbers of the sampan were immersed in the water. Then came the distinct sounds of the burned wreckage breaking up, a fearful racket. Then, all was quiet.

"That's it," said Mills. "She's gone." After another five minutes, he said to Yates, 'Okay, Wally, take the conn. Take her up."

Yates took over, giving orders to surface. Bob Pierpont stuck his head up into the conning tower and said, "Captain, Doc reports that it's a girl! She's all squared away and chowing down on condensed milk."

# CHAPTER EIGHTEEN

*Shark* nosed slowly northward in the darkness. The fog had thinned, but visibility was still poor. At midnight, the twelve-to-four relieved, and Jim Bell took the deck. Despite the fact that Mills or Hunt, or both, came to the bridge every ten minutes or so, Bell felt lonely and not a little fearful. He had never been so close to enemy territory.

"Range to O Shima, one-oh-five-oh-oh," radar reported. Five miles.

"Recommend you come right to zero-three-zero." This was Pierpont in the conning tower.

"Make it so," Bell replied.

"Steering zero-three-zero," said the watch helmsman, Frank Nalle.

Al Weir appeared in the control-room hatch and shouted up to Pierpont, "Tell Mr. Bell that I'm getting a strong intermittent signal on the APR at 153 megacycles. It looks like a land-based radar on Cape Nojima conducting a routine sweep."

The APR was a radar-detecting device that was located in a niche inside the radio shack in the rear of the control room.

"Aye," said Pierpont, and he passed the word to Bell, who responded with instructions to tell the captain.

Pierpont consulted the chart. Nojuma Saki was a cape at the south end of the Boso Peninsula, and formed the right side of the Sagami Sea, or outer Tokyo Bay. The cape was thirty miles distant, not yet on *Shark*'s radar. They knew from reports by boats that had patrolled the area that land-based radar would be encountered on Cape Nojima.

"Battery charge completed," Bill Gilsey, the electrician's mate, reported up the conning-tower hatch.

"Aye," Pierpont said, relaying the message to Jim Bell.

"Light the smoking lamp," Bell said. Smoking was forbidden during the final stages of a battery charge when the hydrogen gas buildup was greatest.

Pierpont took out a cigarette as he passed the word quietly on the PA system: "All hands, the smoking lamp is lit. The smoking lamp is lit."

Hunt came up to the conning tower from the wardroom. He stared at the chart and said, "How's visibility?"

"Better, but still lousy," Pierpont replied, dragging on his cigarette. He put his finger on the chart. "Land-based radar here."

"I got the word."

Hunt climbed up to the bridge. The land odor was now very strong, and he felt a wave of nostalgia.

Bell said, "What are we going to do with that damned baby?"

"Keep it, I guess," said Hunt. "The captain and I were discussing alternatives, like handing it over to another sampan, but that won't do. We'd give away our game."

"You wouldn't believe it in this day and age," said Bell, "but some of the older hands are superstitious about having a female on board. They're convinced it means bad luck."

"Range to O Shima one-two-oh-oh-oh," radar reported. They were opening out, leaving the island on the port quarter.

Childress had been peering into the fog for two hours without letup, and his eyes were beginning to play tricks on him. He thought he saw something; he blinked and looked again, and then he said quietly, "I think there's something in the water. Dead ahead."

Bell reacted instantly. "All back full!"

*Shark* drifted forward another hundred yards. As her screws reversed, the deck trembled, and then she stopped dead in the water.

"It looks like a mine," said Pierpont, his binoculars glued on the object that was now bobbing off the port bow.

Mills hurried to the bridge. "What's up?"

"Our sharp-eyed quartermaster picked up an object in the water," said Hunt.

Mills looked through his binoculars. "It's a glass fishnet ball. A float for the nets."

Childress examined the object through his binoculars. He'd never seen a glass float, but clearly that's what it was.

"All ahead two-thirds," said Bell. "Steer zero-three-zero."

"We better flood down," Mills said. "Make those radar operators on Nojima Saki earn their pay."

"Aye, aye," said Bell. Then to the intercom, "Control. We're going to run decks awash. Vent main ballast to the mark."

"Vent main ballast to the mark, aye," repeated the chief of the watch.

They heard the hydraulically operated vents clanking open, then the hiss of escaping air.

"Rig out the bow planes," said Bell.

They saw the big winglike planes unfold at the bow. Then they heard the vents clank shut.

"Main ballast vented to the mark," control reported. "Bow planes rigged out."

With her main ballast tanks partially filled with seawater, *Shark* settled into the water until the wood-slat main deck was awash. Only her bridge structure and the periscope shears extended above the surface, making her almost impossible to detect by radar.

"I'm going down for coffee," Mills said. "Let me know when you cross into the Sagami Trough." The Sagami Trough was a trench in the ocean floor running northwest-southwest between O Shima and Cape Nojima. The ocean depth in the trench was four thousand feet.

"Aye, captain."

As Mills turned to duck below, he paused and said to Childress, "That black eye didn't seem to hurt you any. Good work."

Five minutes later, radar reported, "Aircraft! Bearing zero-zero-zero. Range one-oh-oh-oh-oh." Five miles.

"Constant ranges and bearings," Bell ordered. They wouldn't dive unless attacked. With the poor visibility, they weren't apt to be spotted by aircraft.

"Range opening out. One-five-oh-oh-oh," radar reported.

"Very well," said Bell with an inward sigh of relief. The planes would be no threat. Not those, anyway.

An hour later they crossed into Sagami Trough. When notified, Mills gave orders to dive. Bell cleared the bridge, and when he was certain that all hands were below, he sounded the diving alarm and jumped down the hatch. In her flooded-down state, *Shark* descended quickly, and they leveled off at two hundred feet.

The watch sonar operator reported to Bell, "Sir, there's an odd noise coming from dead ahead. I think it's a shipboard noise."

Bell held the earphone to his right ear. Yes, it was odd. A high-pitched squeal. He telephoned the forward torpedo room, and the watch torpedoman answered instantly. Bell said, "We're getting a funny squeal on sonar. Are you guys making it?"

"No, sir," the torpedoman replied. "I was just about to call you. We can hear it. It sounds like it's coming from inside the forward trim tank.

"Very well," said Bell, hanging up, puzzled and worried as he sent the watch messenger to inform the captain. This was no place for mechanical casualty. Japanese sonar would pick up a squeal like that from miles away.

# CHAPTER NINETEEN

Chief Petty Officer Cecil Kilpatrick, the senior motor machinist's mate, laid out the heavy sheaf of blueprints on the wardroom table. Kilpatrick, an old, old hand, had the finest mechanical mind on *Shark*. He had defined the squeal as escaping air, and he had isolated it to the forward trim tank. The squeal had set in when they dropped to two hundred feet, but the cause of it had Kilpatrick momentarily baffled; he'd never run into anything like it before. Together, he and Mills poured over the blueprints of the trim and drain system, speculating, kicking the problem around.

After a time, Kilpatrick tapped his pencil point on one section of the blueprint. "See that flange, there, captain? Where the bow plane rigging rod goes through the tank? I have a hunch the leak's there."

"Why?" Mills asked, very much on edge. That squeal could mean disaster. Unless it was promptly repaired, he would be compelled to abort the mission, a humiliating finish to his career on *Shark*.

"The flange opens to sea," said Kilpatrick. "It's the only place air *could* be leaking."

"Mmmmmmmmm," said Mills, studying a side

view of the flange. It was held in place by eight big bolts.

"I'll bet someone took that flange off during refit and forgot to tighten those bolts when they put it back on," said Kilpatrick. "Now they've worked loose."

"What can be done about it?" Mills asked impatiently.

"Pump out the tank, put a couple of men inside, dive, and check it out."

"But if they find you're right, how can it be fixed?" Mills pressed.

"Put a man overboard in the superstructure. The nuts are on the outside. Tighten the nuts."

"Mmmmmmm," said Mills with a sinking feeling. The odds on fixing that leak were long, very long.

"Who'll we put in the tank?" Mills asked. The idea of entering that tank was appalling.

"Two very brave, skinny guys," Kilpatrick said, grinning. "Me, for one. I'll find a volunteer."

Kilpatrick returned in five minutes. "I've got the other man, captain," he said.

"Who?" Mills said eagerly.

"Willie the Silent," Kilpatrick said.

"How did you know he volunteered?"

"He raised his hand."

"You and Willie fix that leak, and you both get a gong—and a promotion."

"I'll take the gong, captain, but no promotion. If you promote me to warrant, I'll have to leave submarines."

"Well, that's true," Mills said, reconsidering. "Okay. No promotion."

They marked time in the Sagami Trough all day, remaining at one hundred feet. Sonar reported many ship screws during the day, but they didn't even come up for a periscope observation. It was like a holiday for the off-duty watch standers. No drills. No battle stations. Childress completed five more diagrams for his qualification notebook. Seven men were eliminated from the cribbage tournament. After lengthy consultations with Pops Wheeler on baby care, Tony Walker made a bassinet for Lockwood-san in the after torpedo room. He fashioned a bottle, and every four hours he fed her condensed milk thinned with water.

After dark, at 1921, they surfaced in dense fog midway between Nojima Saki and O Shima. Radar reported no unusual contacts. The sea was calm, and for that they were thankful. A rough sea would have made repairs impossible.

Mills himself took charge of the trim tank inspection team. He, Kilpatrick, Willie Bonsel, and two motor machinists climbed down on deck and went forward. The two machinists removed the topside manhole cover from the trim tank, and Kilpatrick and Bonsel, carrying tools and two flashlights, squeezed down through the small opening into the tank. The machinists bolted the manhole cover back in place, then followed Mills back to the bridge.

Mills spoke into the intercom. "Control, bleed air into the forward trim tank."

"Pressure in the tank," Pops Wheeler returned. "Holding." That meant the tank was watertight.

"Okay, Pops," Mills said. "Stand by to dive."

"Standing by to dive."

Mills supervised the dive, taking *Shark* to a hundred feet. Then he went to the forward torpedo room where a crowd had gathered. A torpedoman striker had manned the sound-powered telephone. Mills climbed down into the bilge and hit the side of the trim tank with a hammer, a prearranged signal, telling the men inside the tank that *Shark* had reached one hundred feet. In response, he heard two clangs. That meant all was well, go deeper. "Two hundred feet," Mills said to the man on the telephone, who relayed the order to the control room. *Shark* nosed down. At two hundred feet, the high-pitched squeal set in. They could hear it plainly in the torpedo room. It was unnerving.

Mills counted the seconds ticking away. Everything depended on the skill and courage of Kilpatrick and Bonsel. Presently, he heard four metallic clanks. His heart leaped. That signal meant they had found the leak! It was the flange, after all.

"Surface," Mills said to the telephone talker, who relayed word to the control room. Almost instantly, the surface alarm sounded: *Aauuuuugah. Aauuuuugah. Aauuuuugah.* As the bow lifted sharply and high-pressure air hissed into the ballast tanks, Mills went aft to the control room, then up to the conning tower. When *Shark* broke water, Mills undogged the hatch and went up to the bridge.

"All clear starboard," a lookout sang out.

"All clear port," another shouted.

Mills, trailed by the two machinists, went on deck to the trim-tank manhole cover. When the machinists removed the cover, Bonsel was first out of the tank. As usual, he had nothing to say. Then Kilpatrick appeared, saying, "It's the flange bolts, all right, captain."

"Good work," said Mills, putting an arm around each of their shoulders and escorting them to the bridge.

Kilpatrick handpicked a detail to tighten the flange bolts. The key man was Gunner's Mate Tony Walker, who was also the ship's unofficial diver. He put on a shallow-water diving mask, descended into the water inside the superstructure, and with a big wrench provided by Kilpatrick, he tightened the eight bolts. It was an enormously difficult task, carried out in confined space underwater. When he finished, Walker was so exhausted that he had to be helped up on deck.

Now they were ready for the big moment. Had

they fixed the casualty? Once again, Mills supervised the dive. He stood in the conning tower at the sonar stack, chewing his nails. Kilpatrick stood beside him, confidently.

'Two hundred feet," Mills ordered, and they went slowly down.

When the depth gauge needle indicated two hundred feet, Mills held the sonar earphones to his ear. He could hear nothing; the squeal was gone. He beamed and turned to Kilpatrick, slapping him on the back. "Chief, you're a bloody genius."

Kilpatrick grinned.

"Okay," Mills said to the officer of the deck, "take her up."

He went below and found Doc Jones. "Issue a ration of medicinal brandy to Kilpatrick, Bonsel, Walker, and the other men in the work party," he said.

To Hunt, in the wardroom, he said, "Best goddamn crew in the whole goddamn navy."

Hunt did not doubt his words.

## CHAPTER TWENTY

Running decks awash, they left Nojima Saki on the starboard quarter. It was past midnight. The narrow funnel-shaped passage to Tokyo Bay, Uraga Suido, lay ten miles dead ahead. The passage and the surrounding peninsulas, as well as the lower, inner bay, were clearly outlined on the radarscope.

Mills stared at the geographical features displayed on the radarscope. He knew from charts, maps, sailing directions, and gazetteers that the shoreline of Tokyo Bay was one vast urban sprawl. One city linked to the next: Tokyo, Kawasaki, Yokohama, Yokosuka. There were probably fifteen million Japanese living in those cities, and together this comprised the principal manufacturing center of the Japanese war machine. It would have been comparable to having New York, Detroit, Toledo, Gary, and Philadelphia rolled into one vast metropolis.

Mills returned to the wardroom where Hunt sat at the table studying charts and intelligence documents on Tokyo Bay.

Mills said, "We're approaching Uraga Suido."

Hunt nodded. He didn't have to be told, for he was following *Shark's* creeping, cautious progress almost yard by yard.

Mills fell to work on a chart of Uraga Suido and marked off distances with a pair of dividers. Then he looked at his watch. "I'd say pull the cork in about one hour."

"Yes," said Hunt, picking up a piece of paper on which Pierpont had jotted his own recommendations. They all coincided.

For the tenth time that day, Mills turned to Hunt's report on the antisubmarine net. It was a remarkable document both for its simplicity and clarity and for the wealth of its technical data.

The net spanned the main channel of Uraga Suido at a point where the channel—and the traffic route—made a left turn to the northwest, to swing around a jut of land known as Huttu Saki. The net ran north-south across the channel, between two old forts—Daini Kaiho and Daisan Kaiho—and it was 2,500 nautical yards long, about a mile and a quarter. There were minefields planted between Daini Kaiho and the shore and Daisan Kaiho and the shore, forcing all ship traffic to use the main channel.

The net itself was a remarkable engineering

achievement. Made of squares of quarter-inch steel cable, it was suspended from a train of twenty-foot pontoons. Where the cable spanned the main channel, the water was about 120 feet deep, and the net hung down to 80 feet, deep enough so that no submarine could squeeze beneath it. In its center was a "gate" a hundred feet wide, operated by two net-tending vessels.

Mills laid aside the report and studied the detailed chart of their objective: the Yokosuka Naval Base. The base lay about three nautical miles due east of the net. It was situated among a maze of channels, inlets, and islands, seemingly hacked out of rocky cliffs. At the center of the base, there was a large hilly island Azuma Hanto, used for storing fuel oil and ammunition. Mills noted that the two large hills on the island rose to 226 and 288 feet. The water between the net and the naval base was deep, averaging 30 fathoms, or 180 feet, and just off the base itself, the water in the main outer anchorage was 15 fathoms, or 90 feet, more than enough to conceal *Shark*.

"You're sure there are no minefields between the net and the base?" said Mills.

Hunt gave the answer he had given twice before. "Captain, the code breakers claim to have good info on minefields, picked up from Jap notices to mariners. To the best of their knowledge, there are no minefields between the net and the base."

"How late was their info?" Mills asked.

"Not more than ninety days old."

"A field could have been planted since then."

"But why," said Hunt, "would it be inside the submarine net?"

"All the better reason," Mills said. "The Japs got inside our nets at Majuro and Eniwetok with that new weapon, whatever it is. If they can do it, they'll be assuming we can do it, too. You make a new weapon, you also make a defense against it."

"Well, of course," Hunt said, reconsidering. "That's a good point."

"So we'll have to be very careful. Not assume anything."

"Yes, sir," said Hunt, watching Mills closely. Mills was wholly absorbed in the mission, his concentration total.

## CHAPTER TWENTY-ONE

They dived at 0210, within the Uraga Suido channel, a little south and east of Kannon Saki. They were five miles south of the net in 225 feet of water. To reach the net, they had merely to go due north about two and a half miles, turn left at Kannon Saki, follow the main channel, and then proceed the remaining two and a half miles on a northwest course. At slow speed, against the outgoing tide, it would take them about two hours. Mills's plan was to survey the net at close range in morning twilight, withdraw about a mile to await a large incoming vessel, and slip in beneath the larger vessel when the gate opened.

They trimmed the boat and proceeded up the channel at radar depth, thirty-five feet, making about two knots per hour. In the conning tower, Mills manned the periscope, Weir was at the radar, and Hunt and Pierpont plotted their course. Mills was astonished to find a lighted navigation beacon on Kannon Saki, and they used it to take a bearing.

At 0315, when Kannon Saki Light was directly off the port beam, they came left to a bearing of 320—northwest. The net gate was now dead ahead, a little less than three miles away. Mills could see the running lights of the net-tender vessels. Ten minutes later the moon rose over Boso Peninsula.

"Half-moon," Mills muttered at the periscope, watching it rise over the rugged mountains to the east.

"Radar contact!" Al Weir said quietly, galvanizing them all. "It looks like a really big ship coming out of Tokyo, range one-two-oh-oh-oh."

"Very well," said Mills.

"Another big ship behind it," said Weir. "Really huge. Never seen pips like these."

"It's not land or some kind of echo?" asked Mills, still at the periscope.

"No. They're moving. Very fast."

Mills noted activity on one of the net-tending vessels. Signal lights, a puff of smoke from the stack. "I think they're coming out," he said.

"And we're right in the middle of the channel," Hunt reminded him from the chart desk.

"They're opening the gate," Mills said, tempted to put on full speed and dash through.

"They're really barreling along," Weir said, hypnotized by the two huge pips. "Range nine-oh-oh-oh."

"Very well," said Mills. "We better get out of the way. All ahead standard. Come right to zero-four-zero."

*Shark* turned right and picked up speed.

"Take a sounding," Mills ordered.

"Forty-two fathoms," control responded. Two hundred fifty-two feet.

"Range seven-five-oh-oh," said Weir.

Hunt walked over and looked at the pips. They were indeed enormous. Battleships or carriers, he thought.

"I can just make out the lead ship," said Mills, staring at her top-hamper in the moonlight. "The gate is open. She's coming through. She's big, all right. Looks like a battlewagon."

"Captain," said Pierpont, "we're out of the channel, headed for shoal water."

"All stop," said Mills. "Left full rudder."

They swung left and drifted to a stop.

"Sounding," Mills said.

"Twenty fathoms," control reported. One hundred twenty feet.

"Take her down to periscope depth," said Mills. "Secure the radar."

Weir turned off the radar, secured the antenna, and they dropped down to sixty feet. All the while, Mills stared through the periscope cross hairs at the onrushing vessels. "First one's going through the gate now," he said, "and here comes the other one."

He could see both vessels plainly in the moonlight. "My God!" he said. "They're gigantic. Have a look, Bill."

Hunt took the periscope. It was fixed on the lead ship. Enormous! Huge bow wave and massive top-hamper. Big, big guns and turrets. The identity of the vessels occurred to him at once. "Captain! It must be *Yamato* and *Musashi!*"

*Yamato* and *Musashi* were the largest warships ever built—sixty thousand tons each—designed and constructed entirely in secret during the late 1930s. Each mounted nine eighteen-inch guns plus a host of smaller batteries—more firepower than any ships in history—and they had not been known to the U.S. naval authorities or the code breakers until after the Battle of Midway in June 1942, when both ships were employed to escort the abortive Midway Invasion Force. Since that time, only scant bits and pieces of intelligence had been accumulated on them. There was a rumor that a third sister ship had been completed and was being converted into a giant aircraft carrier, but this had not been verified.

Mills returned to the periscope to continue his surveillance. As *Yamato* swept by at close range, they could hear the thunderous beat of her screws.

Mills was nearly beside himself. "Bill," he said. "if we got one of those babies, it would mean a hell of a lot more than this Mickey Mouse mission."

"I heard they've got armor a foot thick," said Hunt. "Torpedo-proof."

"We could sure scare the hell out of them," Mills insisted, swinging the cross hairs to *Musashi*. "Angle on the bow, twenty port. Jesus! What a perfect setup."

He stepped back from the periscope. "What say, Bill?"

"Your decision, captain."

Mills was thinking: What a swan song for Mauler Mills! Ten solid hits in *Musashi*! He shook his head. In these waters, an attack would be suicidal.

For the next ten minutes—until the extraordinary ships pulled out of sight—Mills kept the periscope fixed on first one and then the other as he rattled off a continuous litany of technical information, which Pierpont jotted down. This would be useful for Admiral Nimitz and his staff, for no one had ever seen the ships close up like this.

When the ships had passed, Mills shook his head in disappointment. Opportunities for submarine attacks on Japanese battlewagons were rare, and the sub force had never seriously damaged a battleship. He had passed up an opportunity to damage two of Japan's most valuable vessels. Wait until Admiral Lockwood got *that* news.

"Radar depth," said Mills.

They came back up to thirty-five feet, and Weir turned on the radar.

"Left full rudder," Mills said. "All ahead two-thirds."

*Shark* swung around and once again closed on the net at creeping speed. Morning twilight was approaching, and Mills could now make out the net-tending vessels. Old wooden ships, resembling minelayers. They would probably be equipped with sonar, he thought, but the operators probably lacked talent. The best sonar operators were assigned to the Imperial Fleet, and that policy might work to Shark's advantage now.

"Radar contact," Weir said. "Looks like a ship coming up the channel behind us. Range seven-oh-oh-oh."

Mills turned to Hunt. "Let's not wait around," he said. "If this looks right, let's go on in and get it over with."

"Good idea, captain," said Hunt. "The sooner, the better."

"Go to battle stations," Mills ordered.

"Range six-five-oh-oh," said Weir. "I'd guess she's doing about nine knots."

"Very well," Mills said.

"All hands at battle stations," Pierpont reported.

"Up scope," Mills said.

Sweeping the scope around, Mills began to make out details on shore: houses, telephone poles, bridges, hills, rugged cliffs. There was a light chop on the water. It would help camouflage the periscope feather.

"Range five-oh-oh-oh," Weir said.

"I see her now," said Mills. "She's rounding Kanagawa Point. Big old rusty freighter. In ballast. Angle on the bow ten port. Mark bearing!"

They set the ship up on the TDC as though it were a target. This would help Mills choose the proper intercept course. He said to sonar, "Stay on the freighter. Give me continuous bearings."

Doc Jones complied. The freighter was around the point now coming dead on, steady on three-two-zero. Mills maneuvered Shark until he was on a parallel course, off to one side of the freighter's track.

"We'll let her go by and swing in right behind

her," Mills said to Bell and Yates. "Then we'll put on a burst of speed and get directly beneath her."

"Distance to the track five-oh-oh," Bell said. "She's slowing down. Speed estimate seven knots."

Mills took another look at the freighter, lined up the cross hairs on the rusty old-fashioned bridge amidships, and said, "Mark! Down scope. Secure radar. Eighty feet." The freighter was close. The scope would not go up again. From now on, it would all be done with sonar.

"Steady bearing," said Jones. Then, "She's passing us now, captain. Bearing drawing ahead to two-seven-zero."

"All ahead full," said Mills. They could hear the heavy thump-thump of the freighter's screws through the hull. "Right fifteen degrees rudder."

His mind flashed back to the late 1930s, to the war games in Hawaiian waters. In those far-off days (or so they seemed now), it had been believed—and it was sub force policy—that sonar was the most effective method of tracking an enemy. That was long before anyone in the fleet had even heard of radar. As a consequence of this policy, the peacetime sub force had drilled relentlessly in the use of the sonar attack, and given a few sonar bearings and other data, men like Mills could readily picture what was going on.

"Screws slowing down," Jones said. "Merged with net-tender screws."

"All ahead full," Mills said. "Plane down to one hundred feet." That was deep enough to get under the freighter and still leave twenty feet between Shark's keel and the ocean floor.

As they slipped beneath the freighter, her screw noises were frightful. She sounded like a freight train directly overhead.

"All ahead one-third," Mills said. "Steady as you go."

"Screws speeding up," Jones reported, and they could hear and feel the increase in tempo.

"Very well," said Mills.

"Net-tender screws drawing aft," Jones reported. "One-five-zero."

Mills grinned broadly. "We're through the net," he said. "By God, men, we made it!"

They would let the freighter go on now. It had served its purpose. "Left full rudder. Plane up to sixty feet."

At sixty-five feet, Mills knelt for the periscope handles. He exposed only inches of the glass, enough to confirm that they were through the net, inside Tokyo Bay.

"Steady on two-eight-zero," he said to the helmsman. "Down scope." Then to Hunt, "We should have about 120 feet of water in here. Let's take her to the bottom, have breakfast, and get some sleep. We can't do anything in daylight anyway."

"Excellent idea, captain," said Hunt.

"Rig in the sound heads," Mills said. Then to Pops Wheeler in control, "Pops, set her on the bottom gently. About 120 feet."

"On the bottom, aye," said Wheeler.

They planed down, dumping trim water overboard, and they oozed onto the muddy bottom without a sound.

Bill Hunt went below, marveling at the captain's skill and professionalism. It had been Hunt's plan, but it took an old and skilled hand such as Mills to carry it out. He made it seem like a piece of cake. And now, lying on the bottom in the enemy's front yard, Mills had declared another holiday!

# CHAPTER TWENTY-TWO

Like most of the off-watch men, Jack Childress began the morning in his sack, but he could not sleep. He lay for a long time, staring wide-eyed at the coil springs of the bunk over his head, completely unnerved at the thought of being on the bottom of the ocean inside Tokyo Bay. Finally, he concluded he'd better find something to occupy his mind, so he took his qualification notebook to the crew's mess, drew a mug of coffee, and set to work.

There were half a dozen men playing cribbage: Corley and Weaver; Barr and Nutting; Gilsey and Webb. Since the beginning of the tournament, the games had taken on a life-or-death air. Intense, utterly quiet play and a stream of salty language from the losers. There was no mention of where *Shark* was sitting.

Bob Pierpont came into the mess and sat down at the table where Childress was working on a diagram of the Kleinschmidt fresh-water distillers. Pierpont examined the drawing critically. It was good. Childress was indeed a quick study, and there was no doubt he would qualify this patrol. It occurred to Pierpont that maybe Childress should be put in for a promotion to second class. The Old Man was sure to recommend wholesale promotions before he left the boat.

Childress welcomed the interruption. The Kleinschmidt fresh-water distilling system was tedious. He laid his work aside and sipped his coffee.

"Where're you going on your thirty-day leave?" Childress asked, making idle conversation. All the men being transferred off the boat would be entitled to a month's leave in the States.

"Your home state," Pierpont replied. "Miami, Florida."

"I wouldn't go to Miami," Childress said, frowning. "The Air Corps took over the town."

"Yeah?"

"Yeah. All the hotels on Miami Beach are now barracks for men in flight training."

"No shit?"

"No shit," Childress said. "You'd be better off on the west coast of Florida. Naples. Sarasota."

"Are there broads there?"

"Plenty of broads."

"Where're you from?"

"Homestead. A little farming town south of Miami. Just north of Key Largo."

"Are there broads there?" Pierpont asked.

"Not your type, I'm afraid. Country girls, mostly. Very shy. All virgins."

"What about Key Largo?"

"No. Unless you like to fish or goggle dive."

"You a goggle diver?"

"Yes," Childress said, recalling with a twinge of nostalgia his days in the Keys, diving and spearfishing the coral reefs.

"Why didn't you go into the UDT?" Pierpont said.

"I applied," Childress said. "My two choices were first frogmen, second submarines. They sent me to sub school—or so they told me—because they badly needed more volunteers. Big personnel shortage."

Pierpont had heard about that. They were turning out submarines like sausages these days —at Groton, Portsmouth, Mare Island, even a place called Manitowoc, Wisconsin—and they needed thousands of trained volunteers to man them. It was all so different now. Scores of new boats. Statistical war strategies. Fucking BuPers personnel rotation policies.

Childress felt a sharp stab of fear. It was impossible for him to believe he could be sitting like this, talking casually about Florida and girls, with the enemy all around them. He confessed to Pierpont, "I'll be glad when we get out of here. I'm scared shitless."

"You and me both."

# CHAPTER TWENTY-THREE

In the wardroom, Jim Bell and Wally Yates faced another chore: censoring the enlisted men's outgoing mail. The men put the unsealed letters into a slot in the door of Red Weaver's tiny yeoman's shack, and Weaver brought the accumulation to the wardroom once a week for censoring and sealing. It seemed to Bell and Yates that *Shark's* sailors were the most prolific writers in the sub force.

In a way, the two officers found the job fascinating. It provided valuable insights into the minds of the writers—the state of their morale, their problems, their goals. This fact was not lost on the enlisted men. Often they used letters home to air a beef about the boat which they would not otherwise bring to the attention of the wardroom. Since the distribution of the BuPers personnel directive, there had been a prodigious outpouring of letters from those men being transferred. The letters all had a common theme: see you soon!

Bell drew two letters written by Pops Wheeler —one to his wife, one to his daughter. These were always difficult. Wheeler's penmanship and spelling were atrocious. Not even fifth-grade level. Bell read them through, stamped them "Censored," and sealed them.

"Pops has a family problem," he said to Yates, throwing the two letters on the outgoing pile. "Wife's sick. He seems glad he's getting off."

"They ought to beach all those old chiefs," said Yates. "They're too old, too conservative. How old is Pops, anyway?"

"Forty-eight," Bell said.

"Too old for submarine duty."

It had been a recurring debate in the sub force since the beginning of the war. The younger reserve officers, like Yates, as well as some skippers believed that the younger chiefs and ratings should be moved up to positions of responsibility. But Admiral Lockwood believed otherwise and insisted on keeping the old experienced hands, thus blocking the upward promotion of the enlisted men. The new BuPers rotation policy was directly contrary to the admiral's views. In effect, he had been overridden by Washington.

Bell picked up a letter from his radar technician, Al Weir. It was the first letter Weir had written since joining Shark, and it was addressed to a radar technician on another boat. Consumed with curiosity, Bell opened it.

Dear Dave,

How goes life on Albacore?

I was unlucky in one big respect. Shark has the worst quack in the fleet for a pharmacist's mate. I've been ill with what is certainly an attack of appendicitis since we left———. You know what he told me? Take a good shit!

This may be the last you'll ever hear from me. Good luck and good hunting.

Al

"Jesus!" Bell exclaimed. He passed the letter to Yates. "Read *that!*"

Yates skimmed the letter. "Holy smoke!"

"Martinez!" Bell shouted.

The mess steward appeared instantly.

"Ask Doc Jones to get in here on the double," said Bell.

When Doc walked into the wardroom, Bell fixed him with a grave look. "Does Weir have appendicitis?"

"No," Jones said. "Absolutely not."

"What's wrong with him?" said Bell, now recalling Weir's "attack" some nights past.

"I think he has a spastic colon."

"What the hell is that?"

"Nothing serious," Jones said. "Sort of a nervous stomach."

"Are you sure?"

"It's what I think," Jones said. "Sir, ever since that pharmacists's mate in *Destination Tokyo* used bent spoons to operate on that sailor, somebody gets a stomachache and immediately thinks he has appendicitis. I have a memo from the Bureau of Medicine and Surgery predicting this would happen; they gave us specific dope on the symptoms."

"What are you supposed to do if you really do have an appendicitis case?" Bell asked.

"Under no circumstances do we operate," said Jones. "We put them in a rack and pack them in ice."

Mills walked in and sat down. "What's all this?" he said.

"Weir," said Jones with a trace of scorn, "thinks he has appendicitis. I say he doesn't. Weir is your classic hypochondriac.'

"Get Weir in here on the double," Mills said to Jones. Goddamn Weir, he thought.

For once, Weir appeared almost immediately. Mills said, "I hear you think you have appendicitis. Why?"

"I have all the classic symptoms," Weir said, almost disdainfully. "Loss of appetite, nausea, pain. The pain has now localized at McBurney's point. That's critical."

"Mac's *what?*" Mills demanded.

"McBurney's point," Jones interjected. "It's a place down here." He held his lower right stomach. "Appendicitis pain is most intense there." He looked at Weir, wondering where in hell he ever heard of McBurney's point.

Mills turned to Jones. "Have you made a thorough examination of this man?"

"No, sir," Jones said.

"Well, let's do it right now," Mills said, turning to Weir. "Strip to your skivvies and lie down on the table."

Weir did as instructed.

Doc Jones was determined to prove his diagnosis once and for all. There was one simple way. He leaned over and pressed both hands down hard on Weir's upper stomach. Then he let go suddenly, watching Weir's face. He saw no signs of unusual pain. Jones turned to Mills. "Captain, anyone who had appendicitis could not have stood that test. He would have screamed bloody murder. I'm sure what he has is a spastic colon—a stomach upset. I've been treating him with belladonna."

Mills had absolute faith in Jones. He turned to Weir, fighting an impulse to slap him hard. "Get back to your duties."

"But, I—" Weir attempted.

"Shut up, Weir," Mills comanded.

# CHAPTER TWENTY-FOUR

In the after torpedo room, Tony Walker bent over the bassinet. Lockwood-san was smelly again, and Walker changed the diapers he had made out of surplus bunk sheets. Then he fed her a bottle of thinned condensed milk. She drank half the bottle and, cooing contentedly, drifted off to sleep. Walker covered her with a blanket and stared at her with fatherly pride.

He walked forward to the crew's head in the rear of the after battery compartment and put the dirty diaper in a pail to soak with the other diapers. Then he put all the diapers in the Bendix front-loading washing machine, and when they were clean, he hung them on a line in the forward engine room and went forward to the crew's mess for coffee.

Walker had become something of a controversial figure. All on account of Lockwood-san. The signalman, Carl Corley, was his most vociferous critic. Corley had been in the navy since (the joke went) before the Spanish-American War. It was he who had first objected to having a female on the boat, and he maintained that it would bring the worst kind of bad luck.

Walker had never liked Corley. He was a vicious drunk on the beach, he had been busted to seaman countless times, and he had even spent time in the brig for nearly killing a marine in a bar. Lockwood-san had polarized their relationship.

Walker posted a notice on the bulletin board, atop the BuPers directive.

**ALL HANDS**
*Contributions for our mascot Lockwood-san now being collected. Give generously! See Yeoman Weaver.*

*Walker*

Corley read the notice and sneered at Walker. "Contributions? What for?"

Walker was cool. "She'll need clothing and things."

"Well, fuck all that fucking shit," Corley said. He was incapable of talking any other way.

"Blow it out your ass," Walker shot back.

Corley was advancing on Walker menacingly when Pops Wheeler entered the compartment. "Knock it off, Corley," he snapped. "That's an order."

"That fucking female has to go," Corley ranted.

"What do you want to do, fire her out of a torpedo tube?" said Wheeler.

"I don't give a fucking shit how, but she has to get off this boat," snarled Corley.

"Cool it, Corley," Wheeler said, drawing a mug of coffee, "or you go on report."

Corley skulked off. He already had three warnings. One more captain's mast and he'd be back to seaman.

"How's she doing?" Wheeler asked Walker.

"Good," Walker said, beaming. "Her stool's harder now."

"She'll be all right," Wheeler said confidently. "It was probably the drastic change in diet."

"Where does this damned superstition come from?" said Walker.

"From centuries back," Wheeler said. "Probably all the way back to the Phoenicians."

"Well, it's goddamned ridiculous."

# CHAPTER TWENTY-FIVE

At 1609—nine minutes after the four-to-eight watch relieved—Freddie Lyman was helping Johnny Webster bake the daily quota of bread when he heard a light but distinct metal clank on the hull outside the galley. He ran into the control room to report the noise.

In the conning tower, the duty sonar operator, Chuck Vogel, was humiliated. He had been bullshitting with the duty quartermaster and not paying full attention to his job. But he did hear the second and third clanks, and by the time Mills, Hunt, and Pierpont reached the conning tower, Vogel was all ears.

"What was it?" Mills demanded.

"Don't know, sir," said Vogel.

They heard a fourth clank through the hull, directly overhead. It was sharp, louder.

"In the shears," Mills said, looking up.

"Captain," said Vogel, "I think I hear hull noises. No screws. A faint rushing sound."

Mills took the earphones. He had heard noises like that before. "Sailboats," he pronounced.

"Sampans," Pierpont elaborated.

"Fishing?" Hunt speculated. "The clanks could have been the weights on their nets."

"Goddamn," said Mills, again looking up. "I sure hope the nets don't snag on our shears."

"They probably know this bottom like the back of their hands," said Hunt. "If they snag—"

"Screws!" Vogel reported. "Light. Fast."

"A patrol boat?" Mills asked.

"Yes," Vogel said. "Sounds like a Chidori. A torpedo boat."

They waited, not making a sound.

"Slowing," Vogel reported. "Nearly overhead."

Mills leaned down the hatch and stage-whispered to the control room, "Pass the word. Knock off all work. Not a sound."

"Single ping," Vogel reported. "Screw's stopped."

"Shit," Mills said softly.

"Another ping," Vogel said, his voice low.

The dead silence was shattered by a loud metallic blow on the hull.

"Jesus!" said Pierpont. "What the fuck was that?"

They heard a rasping scrape along the hull.

"A grappling hook!" Mills said. "They've fouled their nets on us."

"Screws speeding up," said Vogel. "Pulling away."

"Allah be praised," Hunt said.

"What the hell is going on up there?" said Pierpont.

Mills improvised. "Sampans foul nets and stop, just off the naval base. Navy Chidori comes out to investigate. Offers to help. Pings. Finds nothing Leaves. Fishermen grapple for nets. Cut nets away. Leave."

"We hope!" Pierpont said.

"Up scope," Mills said.

The underwater visibility was poor—an eerie greenish murk. Mills turned the handle to high power and trained the scope on Shark's afterdeck. "It's a net, all right," he said. "Snagged on the deck gun."

"Swell," said Pierpont.

"There it goes," said Mills. "It ripped apart. They're pulling it up. A big chunk of it is wrapped around the gun."

"What do you suppose they're thinking?" Pierpont said. "They fish this bottom for years. Now, today, they snag the nets."

"The question is," said Hunt, "will they report this new and baffling obstruction to the port authorities?"

"I hope we're not around long enough to find out," Mills said grimly.

# CHAPTER TWENTY-SIX

The sun set at 1800, and forty minutes later Mills gave orders to take *Shark* off the bottom. They came up slowly to periscope depth. Mills walked the scope around. It was pitch-dark. He could see nothing.

"Surface," he said quietly.

Mills was first on the dripping bridge. He looked toward shore, toward the base. There were lights everywhere. The land smell was powerful—and repugnant. He went aft to the cigarette deck at the rear of the bridge structure, looked down, and saw the fishnet entangled in the gun. "Send Walker to the bridge with a knife," he said quietly into the intercom.

Walker appeared almost immediately.

"How's Lockwood-san?" Mills asked good-naturedly.

"Coming along fine, sir."

"Good," said Mills. "You'd better hop down there and cut that fishnet away from your gun."

"Aye, captain."

Walker swung down on deck and hurried aft to the four-inch-fifty deck gun. He hacked at the net with the knife until the shreds came free, and then he gathered them up and returned to the bridge, where he paused to look toward land, the naval base, and the lights.

"Goddamn," Walker said softly. "Look at that. Just like Pearl Harbor."

Mills nodded in silent agreement. It was an awesome panorama. "Is the gun free?" he asked.

"All free, sir," Walker said, still hypnotized by the activity ashore. "What should I do with the netting?"

"Keep it for a souvenir," said Mills.

Walker ducked below. It occurred to him that the shreds of netting had value. He would cut them up into small pieces and sell them, donating the proceeds to the Lockwood-san Fund.

Bill Hunt and Bob Pierpont came to the bridge. For a moment they gawked at the lights ashore, and then Mills broke the silence. "All set?"

"All set, captain," Hunt said. They would close the base in darkness, as planned, and submerge.

Mills spoke into the intercom: "Put three engines on the battery charge, make turns on one engine."

"Aye, aye, sir," the conning tower responded, repeating his instructions.

"All ahead one-third," Mills said. "Come left to three-two-zero. Secure the radar."

"Well," Mills said to Hunt and Pierpont with forced cheer, "fasten your safety belts. Here we go!"

# CHAPTER TWENTY-SEVEN

Giving a wide berth to a shallow flat due east of the naval base, *Shark* moved slowly northwest in the inky darkness. Mills had the conn on the bridge, and he was alternating between using his binoculars and the TBT. Every five minutes he ordered a thirty-second radar sweep for navigational purposes. In the conning tower, Pierpont and Hunt worked at the chart desk, meticulously plotting their advance. A slight miscalculation in these dangerous waters could bring instant disaster.

Pierpont was nervous, not himself. He dropped the dividers and knocked his cigarette off the ashtray. He had followed Mills through hell and high water for a long time, and there had been countless unnerving moments, but never anything like this. The tension was almost more than he could bear.

Hunt spoke softly into the intercom: "Captain, we've cleared those flats. Our course now should be two-seven-oh."

"Make it so," Mills replied with monumental calm. "I've got the northeast breakwater light in sight. Stand by. Mark!"

"Two-nine-zero."

"Turn on the radar," said Mills.

Al Weir made a sweep, and Hunt stared at the green display screen. There were ships everywhere. Too many to bother counting. He noted *Shark*'s position. Everything was going according to plan. There was evidently no current in these backwaters, a lucky break.

"Secure the radar," Mills said.

"Secure," Weir replied, turning off the main switch.

Hunt returned to the chart desk. He saw that Pierpont had sweat on his upper lip. No wonder, he thought.

Below, in the control room, Pops Wheeler stood by, sitting on the bow planesman's bench. They were not at battle stations, but Wheeler took it upon himself to back up the chief of the watch. Just in case. A dozen other off-watch personnel had gathered in the control room. There was not one crewman in his bunk.

"All stop!" said Mills, his binoculars fixed dead ahead. "There's something up there, about two thousand yards ahead of us. It looks like a submarine." He shifted to the TBT for a bearing.

"That'll be the main anchorage," Hunt said, measuring off one mile on the chart with the dividers.

"They *are* submarines!" Mills said. "One—two—three—Hell, I can see about a dozen of them. I-class. Moored to buoys."

"Aye," Hunt replied, his heart suddenly surging. So, the code breakers were right again. The I-class boats *were* at Yokosuka in force.

"Secure the engines," said Mills. "Make turns on the battery. All ahead one-third."

"Aye, aye," said Hunt, passing the word to the manuevering room by phone.

They could feel the big diesels shut down, and it was eerily quiet as *Shark* crept forward, her battery supplying power to the screws as if she were submerged.

"Radar," Mills said. "Make a sweep. Give me the range to the breakwater light."

Weir turned on the radar again. Hunt watched the scope over his shoulder. The breakwater could be seen clearly on the display.

"Range one-five-oh-oh." Three-quarters of a mile.

"Mark bearing!" Mills said.

"Two-seven-eight."

Hunt plotted *Shark*'s exact position on the chart with a small neat X. He noted the depth of the water: twenty-five fathoms. One hundred fifty feet. Good.

"I can see those babies clearly," said Mills, his binoculars fixed on the submarines, which were silhouetted by the lights ashore.

"Recommend we pull the cork, captain," Hunt said.

"Okay, Bill," said Mills. "All stop. Stationary dive."

They dived slowly and quietly to periscope depth.

"I didn't see anything unusual about those I-boats," said Mills. "Maybe we ought to take a closer look." He paused. "What's the matter with you, Pierpont? You look like you've seen a ghost."

Pierpont grinned sheepishly and joked, "Combat fatigue, captain. This is making me very, very nervous."

Mills failed to see the humor. "This is our last shot, Bob." he said. "We're down by three points. The ball's on the one-yard line. Third down. Ten seconds left on the clock. We've got to score!"

"Aye, captain," said Pierpont, "but I don't have to enjoy it."

"It's not whether you enjoy the game," Mills continued, "it's whether you win or lose. We're going to win. Period. Up scope. All ahead one-third."

They had no specific plan for after they reached point X. Mills had quite properly said, "We'll play it by ear," and Hunt had assumed they would put *Shark* on the bottom and cautiously come up for periscope observations in daylight. Closing on the moored boats at night was a trifle brash for his taste. But he said nothing.

Glued to the periscope, Mills edged *Shark* to within five hundred feet of the outermost I-boat. He examined the boat through the high-power lens. "Beautiful target," he said. "One fish would finish her off. I can see the deck watch. He's drinking something from a mug."

"Tea," Hunt said, remembering well.

Mills laughed aloud. "He dropped the mug! It went over the side. Clumsy bastard! Down scope." He turned to Hunt. "Can't see much. Blinded by the base lights. Might as well secure for the night."

"Aye," Hunt replied, vastly relieved.

They turned the boat around and crept back

to point X, and Mills ordered the boat to descend to the muddy bottom—150 feet. Then he secured all special details and set the regular watch. Pops Wheeler let out an audible sigh of relief.

Pierpont had a splitting headache, and he went below to the control room. As always, Red Weaver was hungry for details. Pierpont was curt. "We're on the bottom, in their anchorage, three-quarters of a mile off the breakwater."

"Keeerist!" said Weaver, whistling softly, shaking his head.

Pierpont went aft to the crowded crew's mess. He drew a mug of coffee, washed down two aspirins, and glanced at Walker's latest notice on the bulletin board: "Fishnet souvenirs for sale. A five-dollar donation per section." Pierpont couldn't stand the nervous laughter, bravado, and horseplay in the crew's mess, so he went to his bunk in the chief's quarters and lay down. What was happening to him? Was he losing his goddamn nerve?

## CHAPTER TWENTY-EIGHT

Mills sat at his desk with a pen and a tablet of white lined paper. He had intended to begin a report on the mission, but for Mauler Mills writing was almost painful, each word like a drop of drawn blood.

He set the pen down, got up, and paced the confined deck space of his cabin. Long ago, he had convinced himself that he could think better on his feet. He was interrupted by a rap on his bulkhead. It was Hunt with a document in his hand.

"Here's the report on *Yamato* and *Musashi*," Hunt said, handing over the document.

Inviting Hunt to sit at the desk, Mills sat on his bunk and read the report. Like Hunt's report on the submarine net, it was a model of clarity and concision. All the facts and no bullshit.

"You ought to be writing position papers for CNO," Mills said, returning the document. "Beautiful job."

Hunt was pleased. The report had not been difficult. Pierpont's notes had been thorough.

"I was just starting on our special mission report," said Mills, pointing vaguely at the blank tablet.

"You want me to take a preliminary crack at it?"

"I'd appreciate that," Mills said. He paused a moment, then went on. "You know, you've got a lot of gray matter up there."

Hunt was flattered but embarrassed. "Thank you, captain. It's good to know I've finally earned your confidence."

"Not my *full* confidence," Mills said quickly. "Paperwork is one thing. Leadership is another."

"What do you mean by that?"

"I'm talking about courage and combat aggressiveness," Mills said. "Going in harm's way."

Hunt was stung. "You think I'm yellow?"

"Nobody in the sub force is yellow," said Mills, "but I'll tell you this. Too damned many officers have failed in combat. Far too many. They look good on paper, but they get out here and fall on their asses. This is tough duty. You're all alone out here. There's no room for too much caution."

"I see," said Hunt, quietly smoldering as he stood up. "Is that all, sir?"

"Don't take it personally, Bill. This war is not a personal matter."

"Aye, aye, sir."

Seething, Hunt returned to the wardroom. He

recalled his farewell conversation with his former boss, Dick Voge. "Mauler thinks he's a reincarnation of Mush Morton," Voge had said. "Don't let him go off half-cocked." From that, Hunt had concluded that one of his unofficial tasks was to be a balance wheel to Mills, and that was why he had delicately demurred when Mills hungered to attack the tanker convoy. Now Mills doubted his courage. It was infuriating.

## CHAPTER TWENTY-NINE

Since coming off watch at 1600, Jack Childress had been lying in his bunk in the grip of total terror. The idle hours between watches had become an agony for him. He could think of nothing other than his impending death. Tonight he was certain he would not live out the following day.

He got up, went to the crew's mess, and drew another mug of coffee. The mess hall was clean and vacant. Freddie Lyman and Johnny Webster had finished up and turned in—leaving a stack of doughnuts and sweet rolls. Childress glanced at the sweets, but he had no appetite.

Doc Jones, a perennial night owl, came in from the control room, got a mug of coffee, and sat down with Childress. "What's the good word, Jack?"

"Doc, can I get a medical transfer? I don't think I'm psychologically fit for submarine duty."

"What's the matter, son?" said Jones, giving Childress his undivided attention.

"My nerves are shot," said Childress. "I can't sleep. I can barely function."

Jones chuckled. He held his hand out over the table. Even though he was up to four phenobarbitals a day, his fingers trembled. "You ain't alone, Jack."

"I'm serious," Childress pressed. "I feel like I'm jumping out of my skin."

Jones pointed to the coffee mug. "How many of those do you drink in a day?"

Childress stopped to calculate. His estimate startled him. "Maybe ten, twelve cups a day."

"That's a lot of caffeine," said Jones. "No wonder you're jumpy. You probably need sleep. Knock off the coffee for two, three days. I'll give you something to help you sleep."

Jones took a vial from his shirt pocket and shook out half a dozen small white phenobarbitals. "Take two of these before hitting the sack."

Childress looked at the pills skeptically. He had never taken a pill in his life, not even an aspirin, and he said earnestly, "You don't understand, Doc. I'm scared shitless. I'm not suited for this duty. I want a transfer."

"What do you intend to do?" said Jones. "Get off the boat in Tokyo Bay? Look, son there's not a man on this boat who's not scared shitless. Even the Old Man, I'll bet. If you weren't scared shitless, you wouldn't be normal. Now take those pills and hit the sack."

Childress looked at the pills again. He got up, took a sip of water from the scuttlebutt, and washed down two. When he returned to his bunk and climbed in, the pills took effect almost instantly, and he slept like a log.

# CHAPTER THIRTY

As ordered, the watch messenger woke Mills and Hunt at 0500. By that time the crew had begun to stir. Martinez, ever cheerful, served a heaping platter of pancakes and bacon, and as usual, Mills ate as though he were starving.

They went up to the conning tower. In addition to the normal watch standers, Pierpont, Weir, and Doc Jones were on hand; Weir standing by the radar, Jones manning sonar.

"Morning, men," Mills boomed, looking closely at Pierpont. "How you feeling today, Bob? Get some sleep?"

"Not too bad, captain," said Pierpont. "Got a few hours rack time." It had been one nightmare on top of another.

"Well," Mills said, "let's get the job done and get the hell out of here."

"I'll drink to that," Pierpont said.

Jones removed his earphones. "Morning, captain," he said. "You'll be interested to know it's raining up there."

He offered the earphones to Mills and Mills could hear the soft patter on the surface of the water. He returned the earphones. The rain was good; it would provide some cover for the periscope and keep most of the Japanese inside.

"Our lucky day," said Mills. "Okay, take her up to sixty-five feet."

"Heavy screws at zero-five-zero relative," Jones reported. "Closing."

Mills reached for the periscope handles, saying, "Put me on zero-five-zero."

Hunt looked up at the azimuth, swung the periscope to the correct bearing, and the periscope broke water, facing the source of the screws. In the morning twilight and rain, Mills could see the sinister silhouette of an I-boat under way. It looked remarkably like a U.S. fleet boat.

"I-boat," he said. "Angle on the bow fifteen port. She's coming in. Down scope."

The I-boat would have an alert watch on the bridge. Better to let her pass. Mills said, "Eighty feet."

They waited, listening through the hull to the I-boat's screws. When the sound had gone, they came back to periscope depth. It was almost sunrise now, and the rain had abated.

Mills made a 360-degree sweep with the periscope, noting the moored I-boats and the docks, warehouses, shops, and cranes at the naval base. "She went right into the finger piers," he said. Focusing on the outermost of the moored I-boats, he could see the deck watch wearing foul weather gear. Speaking aloud, he examined the boat closely: "Two periscopes. Radio antenna. No radar mast visible. Maybe retracted. Or maybe no radar. No TBT. JP-type T-bar sound head on the forward deck. Down scope."

Pierpont was furiously making notes.

Mills scratched his head and said to Hunt, "You suppose they've been called in for a radar retrofit?"

"But why all at once?" said Hunt.

That was the nagging question: Why all at once? Mills remembered two years back when the first SJ radars were installed in the American fleet boats. The boats had not been recalled en masse for a retrofit. The radar, as available, had been installed boat by boat as they returned from war patrol. Surely the Japanese would follow the same procedure. No. It must be something else.

"Okay," said Mills. "Let's creep in closer."

Hunt checked the chart. He and Mills had drawn a red line running north-south from the tip of the breakwater to the main base. It was a little over one mile from the red line to the base: 2,300 yards. The water at the line averaged twelve fathoms—seventy-two feet. Submerged, they could get no closer, and even that was calling it close.

"All ahead one-third," said Mills. "Steer two-seven-zero."

"I've got screws all over the dial," Jones reported.

"Secure sonar," said Mills. "Rig in the sound heads. Seventy feet."

*Shark* moved toward the base at two knots, skirting to the north of the main anchorage where the I-boats were moored. One hour later, Mills said, "All stop. Sixty-five feet."

When the periscope came up, Hunt set it on the estimated bearing for the breakwater light. Looking into the scope, Mills said, "Christ! It's raining cats and dogs again. There's the breakwater light. Mark! Here comes a liberty boat. Down scope. All stop."

Hunt plotted the bearing. They were exactly at the predicted position on the red line.

"Control!" Mills shouted. "Take a single sounding."

They heard the sharp metallic *ping* of the machine, but with all the underwater noise in the harbor, Mills was certain it would not be noticed.

"Twelve fathoms, sir."

They heard light screws passing overhead off the port beam. "That's that liberty boat," Mills said. Then, "All right, gentlemen, let's get to work. The camera, please."

Pierpont had the camera loaded and ready, and he slipped it into the periscope slot.

"Put me on the extreme left side of the base,"

Mills said as the periscope came up. He put the scope in high power, clicked the shutter, moved the scope a degree or two to the right, and clicked again. He continued this until the scope had reached the extreme right side of the base. Then he removed the camera, and Pierpont lowered the scope.

"Have Titus develop that right away," Mills said needlessly to Pierpont. Then to control, "Take her to the bottom."

Titus was standing by in the control room. He removed the roll of film from the camera and hurried to the forward torpedo room where he had set up a makeshift darkroom. He developed the film, put it in an enlarger, and made prints of each frame. When the prints were dry, he took them to the wardroom and laid them on the table, where Hunt, Mills, and others were waiting with magnifying glasses.

"Well, shit!" said Mills. "Worst bunch of pictures I've ever seen."

The prints were badly underexposed, murky and muddy. "Not enough light," Mills grumped. "Let's go up again. I'll eyeball it."

When the periscope broke water, it was again fixed on the extreme left of the base. Moving the scope slowly clockwise, Mills called out what he saw. "Still raining like hell. Okay, at number one finger pier—one, two, three, four, five, six, seven I-boats. Machine shop behind. Lot of arc welding going on. Crane is lowering something big onto an I-boat. Finger pier number two. Light cruiser. Destroyer. One, two three, four, five, six, seven I-boats. Christ what a target! One tugboat, one small oiler, and a garbage scow. Finger pier three. Heavy cruiser. One, two, three, four, five I-boats. More welding. Lots of activity on I-boat decks. Here comes another liberty launch. Down scope."

The liberty launch passed to starboard, and ten minutes later Mills put up the scope again and continued his reconnaissance and oral report. Pierpont took reams of notes.

At 0650, Mills concluded his observations, took another bearing on the breakwater light, and ordered the boat to the bottom. Then he took Pierpont's notes and the chart and went to the wardroom.

# CHAPTER THIRTY-ONE

Cecil Kilpatrick, the chief motor machinist, stuck his head in the wardroom. "You wanted to see me, captain?"

Kilpatrick sat down at the table beside Jim Bell. Others present were Wally Yates and Bill Hunt.

"I'd like you to help us puzzle out what we're seeing up there," Mills said to Kilpatrick. Then to Hunt, "Okay. Review."

Holding Pierpont's notes, Hunt said, "We've counted a total of thirty-four I-boats in Yokosuka. It seems clear that this large number of submarines has been called here for a specific purpose, something requiring the services of an elaborate navy yard. That they have brought all these boats here at one time indicates a matter of some moment. Whatever is being done, it's being done *all at once*. And if the work is being done in hard rain, it must be urgent, high priority." He turned to Kilpatrick. "The captain saw intense activity on the boats in the finger piers—a crane was lowering something big onto one of the boats, and a lot of arc welding was going on. Other than that, we don't have a clue."

Kilpatrick nodded. Pierpont had already told him about the crane and the welding. Everyone on the boat knew, and a session not unlike this one had been going on in the crew's mess when he had passed through.

"Well, to state the obvious," said Kilpatrick, "I'd guess it was some sort of heavy external structure modification."

"Yes, but what the hell could it be?" Mills demanded.

Wally Yates raised his hand. "Captain, do I recall correctly that in the late twenties we modified an old S-boat to carry an aircraft stored in a waterproof hangar on deck?"

"Yes," said Mills. "The S-1. Admiral Christie commanded that boat. He told me all about it. They kept the plane in knockdown condition in a big round tank on the deck. They'd put the wings and floats on the plane and let her float off the deck and then take off. But it was a complete fiasco because it was too hard to put the plane together on a pitching deck."

"Might the Japanese be doing something like that with the I-boats?" said Yates. "They're much bigger and more stable than the S-boats were."

"That's a possibility, Wally," said Hunt, making a note.

Yates went on, warming to his idea. "Say the Japs decided to try to close the Panama Canal after all. They equip a force of I-boats with planes, and they launch their planes simultaneously in a surprise attack on the canal."

"By God!" Mills exclaimed. "You might have something, Wally." Like most naval officers, Mills had never understood why the Japanese had not tried to destroy the canal in the early days of the war when the Imperial Fleet controlled the Pacific.

"I don't think so," said Bell.

Mills turned to him. "Go on. Why, Jim?"

"The immediate threat to Japan, the gravest

menace they face, is the U.S. Pacific Fleet," said Bell. "When you're under pressure in war—or anywhere else—you always deal with the immediate threat. The canal should have been closed off early in the war, and now it's not a clear and present danger, merely a strategic sort of threat. I doubt they'd commit practically their whole submarine force to a long-range operation like that. My guess is that whatever's being done, it's something to enable them to go after our fleet."

Mills had to agree with his logic. He kidded, "Jim, you're a muleheaded SOB. You shoot down the only suggestion we have." He turned to Kilpatrick. "Any ideas, chief?"

"I'll have to agree with Mr. Bell," said Kilpatrick. "It's gotta be something like that. Maybe they're beefing up their torpedo capacity. Maybe installing deck torpedo tubes like those on *Narwhal* and *Nautilus*."

*Narwhal* and *Nautilus* were two huge experimental fleet boats designed in the late 1920s. In addition to the typical internal torpedo tubes fore and aft, each boat had four additional tubes topside.

"That's a possibility," said Hunt, making another note. Then a light clicked on in his mind. "I wonder if there could be any connection between the I-boats and that dispatch we got about *Florida* and *Osage*. Quote, Strong probability Japs have new secret naval weapon. Utmost concern on highest levels, unquote."

Mills mulled over the idea. "By God, Bill, you may have a point." Why hadn't they made the connection earlier? Too much to think about. "But I don't understand one thing. Surely no I-boat got through our nets at Majuro and Eniwetok."

"No," Hunt said. "No way. The water is much too shallow to slip in under a ship like we did."

"That's what I mean," said Mills. "So where

does that leave us? If the I-boats are related to a new naval weapon—something that obviously got through the nets—what the hell could it be?"

No one had the slightest idea. They fell silent for a moment and Mills concluded the meeting. "By God, men, we're onto something big,' and we're going to stay right here until we find out what's up. When that rain stops, we'll go up for more pictures."

## CHAPTER THIRTY-TWO

Doc Jones rapped on the bulkhead next to the curtained opening of the captain's cabin.

Mills boomed out, "Come in!"

"May I have a moment, captain?" said Jones, closing the curtain behind him.

Mills tossed aside his ragged paperback, *Untamed Ecstasy*, and sat up on his bunk.

"Sure, Doc. What's up?"

"I'm worried about the crew, captain. I'm not sure how much more of this they can take."

"You mean Pierpont?"

"Not just him, sir," said Jones. "Hell, it's just about everybody. Pops in particular. I just took his blood pressure. It's through the overhead. Two hundred over one twenty."

Wheeler's blood pressure had been above normal for months, but it was never this high.

"He's got a bad family problem," said Mills. "Something's wrong with his wife. That's probably the reason for his high blood pressure. Can you give him something?"

"I've got nothing to give him other than phenobarbital," said Jones, "and I doubt that would do any good. What he needs is to lose about forty pounds."

"Well, put him on a diet."

"He won't *stay* on a diet," said Jones. "Captain, it's not his family problem. It's—well, it's—he needs a rest, a good long blow on the beach. He's been under strain too long. Now this . . ." He waved his hands in the air vaguely.

"He's going to get a rest," said Mills. "He goes off at the end of this patrol."

"I know, sir, but . . ."

Mills stared at his pharmacist for a long beat. Then he exploded. "What do you want me to do, Doc? Cancel the mission because a few of the men are nervous? For Christ's sake, don't you know there's a war on? I'm nervous *too*."

Jones sat still, carefully watching his captain. Days ago he had noted the strange vacant look in Mills's eyes. The look spelled fatigue—long-term fatigue. Mills needed a rest, too. All the old hands did.

Mills broke the awkward silence. "Sorry, Doc. Didn't mean to land on you like that. I guess I'm jumpier than I thought."

"That's all right, captain," said Jones. "You know we're backing you all the way, like always. But, sir, I have to agree with that BuPers directive. I've made my own little study. Five war patrols—especially five Mauler Mills war patrols —are enough for any man. To tell you the honest-to-God truth, I'll be glad to get a rest myself."

Mills was silent a moment, then he stood and put his arm around Jones's shoulder. "Maybe you're right, Doc. Things have changed. It's not like the old days anymore."

"No, sir," said Jones. "It sure isn't."

# CHAPTER THIRTY-THREE

At 1410, when the rain stopped, they came to periscope depth and exposed another roll of film. Titus again made large prints. The light was good, the prints much better. Mills, Hunt, Bell, Yates, and Chief Kilpatrick spread them on the wardroom table in panoramic sequence and studied them under magnifying glasses. They were an amazing set of pictures, but they still shed no clue on the mystery.

After a full hour of close examination of the prints, Mills said impatiently, "Well, this is not getting us anywhere." He turned to Kilpatrick. "Right, chief?"

"I dunno, captain," Kilpatrick replied. "I sure have a better feel for the place. I've still got this gut feeling that it's something to do with torpedoes, even though I don't see anything here to confirm that. Just a hunch."

Mills nodded. He had long ago learned to respect Kilpatrick's hunches. The man definitely had an uncanny mechanical intuition. He said to the group, "Anybody else go along with the chief?"

No one said a word. Mills let the silence hold another moment, then he said, "It doesn't make sense to me. Grant they *do* have beefed-up torpedo capacity tubes on deck, like the chief says, but nobody has explained to me how an I-boat got through our net."

They all remained silent, staring down at the prints.

"Well—back to the drawing board," said Mills.

As the others got up to leave, Hunt said, "Captain, may I speak to you privately?"

"Sure, Bill."

They went to his cabin and pulled the curtain.

"Captain," said Hunt, "I don't think we should sit here much longer. Our exposure is enormous, and the men are under severe tension."

"You, too?" said Mills, his anger rising.

"Wait a minute, please," Hunt shot back. "Hear me out."

"Go on," Mills said sullenly.

"I haven't told you this," said Hunt, "but I was born and raised in Tokyo."

"*What?*" Mills was astonished.

"Yes," Hunt went on. "My father was in the import-export business here. He was also doing some work for the Office of Naval Intelligence. I suspect these charts we're using were produced by him, as well as lots of other stuff. Dad's contact in ONI persuaded him—and me—that I should go to the Naval Academy, so the family returned to the States in 1932. I still speak Japanese fluently."

"Well for Christ's sake!" Mills stared in wonderment at his exec.

"That's one reason Voge shanghaied me to his staff," Hunt went on. "Among other duties, I was Voge's liaison with the code breakers, the translation section. They're good at the language, but they didn't know all the idioms."

"I see," said Mills, flabbergasted. He wondered what was coming next.

"To get to the main point, captain," Hunt continued, "if you could put me ashore somehow, I think I could solve our mystery."

"Put you ashore?" echoed Mills. "Ashore? You mean on the base? Bill, that's crazy. Madness!"

"I think I can get away with it," said Hunt. "It's such an offbeat idea, it just might work."

Mills fell silent, staring at Hunt. Of all people on earth to volunteer for such a risky job . . .

"What if you were caught?" Mills said. "Christ, you're fully briefed on code breaking, the most sensitive secret we've got. They'd get it out of you."

"No," Hunt said. "I've got a pill for that contingency."

"Oh."

"And for the same reason, they would never find out where I came from—but I don't intend to get caught."

"No," Mills said after a time. "It's a gutsy call. But I can't approve it."

"It would be very important to the U.S. Navy," said Hunt. "Perhaps decisive."

"I know that," said Mills, "but we'll find another way."

"I don't think we will," Hunt said. "The problem is simple. We've gone as close as we can go. We've got to get in closer."

After another silence, Mills said, "What's your plan?"

Hunt produced the chart of Yokosuka. "See this island, Azuma Hanto, right off the base? There's a 226-foot hill here, overlooking the finger piers. The beach on our side of the island is deserted—a cliff. If you could launch me in the rubber dinghy at the breakwater, it'd only be a mile and a quarter to the island. In darkness, I could row that distance without being seen, land on the island, conceal the boat, set up an observation point on top of the hill, and return the next night."

He continued for another fifteen minutes, laying out the plan in detail. Mills was impressed. It was a good plan. And so crazy it just might work.

"I'll probably regret this the rest of my life," Mills said, "but okay. We'll put you ashore."

"I don't think you'll regret it, captain."

"You ought to take a couple of volunteers who're handy with guns. Walker, for example."

"I wouldn't want to expose anybody else."

"I can understand that," said Mills, "but I insist on it."

"All right."

"If you're caught, don't give us away. Tell them, tell them—"

"I won't give you away. I'll think of a cover."

"Maybe you could take Lockwood-san ashore with you," Mills joked. "Leave her in the bulrushes."

## CHAPTER THIRTY-FOUR

At 2000, when *Shark* surfaced off the breakwater, it was raining hard again. Hunt and Mills went to the bridge for a final conference. Hunt wore black foul weather gear and carried a .45 pistol. His face was smeared with black shoe polish, and he looked like a movie commando.

"All right, Bill, we'll drop you here, we'll pull out into the open waters of the bay and try to get in a battery charge, and then we'll come back and lie on the bottom. Tomorrow, at 2000, we'll surface right here."

"We'll be waiting for you. Right here," said Hunt.

"And if something goes wrong," Mills went on, "we'll try to rendezvous the following night at 2000." He paused. "If you're not here by then, we'll have to go on home. I can't keep the men here more than another forty-eight hours."

"I understand that very well, captain."

"Well," said Mills, "that's about it. Ready?"

"All set," Hunt said with an air of confidence.

Mills spoke quietly into the intercom: "Send Walker and Vogel to the bridge."

"Aye, aye, sir."

Walker came up first. He was dressed and made up like Hunt, and he carried two Thompson submachine guns and three pairs of binoculars. Behind him came Chuck Vogel, similarly decked out and carrying a knapsack.

Mills joshed with Walker. "In all your years in the navy, haven't you learned never to volunteer for anything?"

"Captain, I wouldn't exactly say I volunteered," Walker returned with a grin.

"What about you, Vogel?"

"You know me, sir. Never miss a chance to hit the beach." Chuck Vogel, a notorious liberty hound and Don Juan, had been handpicked by Walker from among twelve volunteers.

"Well, don't try to pick up any girls this trip," said Mills. "You might get more than a dose of clap."

"Aye, aye, sir," said Vogel, also grinning. His sun rose and set on the Old Man.

"Good luck," said Mills, shaking hands with all three. "Okay, move on out."

Hunt, Walker, and Vogel climbed down to the main deck. Walker and Vogel removed the inflatable rubber dinghy from its waterproof canister, unrolled it, and laid it flat on deck. Vogel connected the portable pump and inflated the craft. They loaded the boat with small arms, ammo, binoculars, a knapsack containing spare ammo, emergency rations and a canteen of coffee, a coil of half-inch rope, and the pump. Then they lowered the boat down over the saddle tanks to the water.

Vogel got in the stern, Hunt in the bow, Walker amidships, and they shoved off into the rainy night, Walker silently and expertly working the small oars.

Mills gave a final wave, then spoke into the intercom: "Right full rudder. All ahead two-thirds."

*Shark* made a 180-degree turn, leaving Yokosuka directly astern. Mills said, "Turn on the radar."

"Radar, aye." A moment later, Al Weir said, "All clear on radar."

Mills turned to the OOD, Wally Yates. "Okay, Wally. We're clear of the base. We'll swing north for a couple of miles, then circle for the rest of the night. Charge batteries on all four main engines; use the dinky for propulsion; make a radar sweep every five minutes; and don't hesitate to call me for *anything*."

"Aye, aye, captain," Yates said.

As Mills was ducking under the fairwater for the hatch, he paused and said, "Oh, Wally . . ."

"Yes, sir?"

"Try to keep us inconspicuous, will you?"

"Aye, aye, captain," said Yates. "Get some sack time, sir. I'll keep you informed."

Mills went below to his cabin and lay down. It was a good night for charging batteries in Tokyo Bay. Nobody was apt to be out and about, and the rain would mute the noise of the diesels. He closed his eyes and tried to sleep, but he was consumed with worries about Hunt, Walker, and Vogel. He wasn't happy that they had left the ship: it made him feel tethered, trapped, immobile.

# CHAPTER THIRTY-FIVE

Tony Walker rowed steadily, pacing himself. Hunt lay with his elbows propped on the V-bow gunnels, binoculars under his hood, searching dead ahead. It was useless. He could see nothing. Seldom had he known a night so dark.

Two minutes later they crashed softly onto a rock ledge. Hunt looked at his watch. Thirty-two minutes had elapsed since they left *Shark*. Hunt held the dinghy off the ledge while Walker shipped the oars. Then all three men slipped over the side into the waist-deep icy water. They heaved the dinghy onto the ledge and climbed out of the water, and while Walker and Vogel deflated the boat, Hunt took a quick survey.

The cliff rose above them, and from what he could see in the dark and rain, it was steeper than he had estimated from the chart. Almost vertical. They would have to climb it like mountaineers.

"Okay," said Walker, "boat stowed in the bushes." He and Vogel had slung the submachine guns over their shoulders. Vogel carried the knapsack; Walker the coil of rope.

"All right," said Hunt. "Up we go."

Hunt tied one end of the rope around his waist and handed the coil to Walker. He found a foot-and handhold and pulled himself up, inching upward, groping for outcrops as the rain runoff splashed in his face. Thirty-five feet above the ledge, he found a substantial indentation and a rock suitable for anchoring the rope. He tied it off, gave three pulls, and pulling themselves hand over hand up the rope, Walker and Vogel scrambled nimbly up the face of the cliff.

"Take five," said Hunt, puffing. His climb hadn't been easy, and he was not in all that good shape. He stared off into space, thinking, here I am, once more on Japanese soil.

"Okay," he said, glancing at his watch, "let's move on."

The next fifty feet were more difficult. It took Hunt over an hour to scale the distance and tie off the rope again. When Walker and Vogel came up, Hunt declared a ten-minute rest, and while they rested, the rain abruptly stopped and they could hear noises from the base—the chatter of rivet guns, the rumble of big cranes, and the dinging of alarm bells.

Going up was easier now. The slope decreased in angle to about thirty degrees, and they came into a thicket of trees and dense, tough waist-high grass. Slogging on, they stumbled upon a deserted gravel road, crossed it warily, and plunged back into the thicket. A quarter of a mile farther, the thicket ended, and they looked out on a grassy clearing. In the center of the clearing, at the very summit of this part of the island, there was a complete antiaircraft battery: guns, searchlights, tents, all enclosed by sandbags stacked six feet high, and an armed sentry slowly patrolling the perimeter.

"Shit," Walker whispered. They had planned to use this summit for their observation post.

They eased back into the edge of the thicket, and Hunt took out the chart and examined it by the beam of a pen-sized flashlight. South of the summit there was another cliff face, directly overlooking the finger piers where most of the I-boats were tied.

They skirted the clearing to the south, keeping in the shadows of the thicket. All the while, they could hear music from a radio. It had been nearly twelve years since Hunt had heard this music, but he recognized the tune: a sad love story set in ancient times. It brought a flood of memories.

At a point due south of the battery they re-entered the thicket and began to descend. A hundred yards father on, Hunt stopped, holding his breath. The land fell away almost vertically, and directly beneath them lay the I-boat finger piers, machine shops, and barracks. He could see the dazzling sparks of arc welding and the workmen swarming over the I-boats.

"All right," he whispered. "This is good."

Walker and Vogel propped the submachine guns against trees. They sat down in the deep grass, then parted it so they had a view of the base below. They stared through their binoculars for a long time, but in the darkness they couldn't make out what was going on. After a while, Hunt secured the watch and said, "Might as well get some shut-eye."

Walker and Vogel were happy enough at that suggestion. It had been a tedious, tense day. They snuggled into the deep wet grass.

## CHAPTER THIRTY-SIX

At 0345, Jim Bell, who had relieved Wally Yates as OOD, sent word to Mills that the battery charge was completed, and a few minutes later, Mills appeared on the bridge. The rain had stopped; the front had passed on; and there wasn't a cloud in the sky.

"Guess we better run back in now and pull the

cork," said Mills. "I'll take the conn, Jim. You bring me in."

Jack Childress was on the bridge, standing to one side, and he followed Bell below to help navigate *Shark* back to the breakwater. As he worked, he had a sinking feeling in his chest, dreading the thought of returning to that shallow water in the enemy's front yard.

Using the radar sparingly, they crept through the darkness to a point two miles due east of the breakwater light. At 0500, they secured the battery charge and dived. By 0600, they had reached the breakwater. They planed down to the bottom and Mills went to his cabin to try to sleep.

Queuing for the second breakfast setting in the mess, Bob Pierpont stood behind the torpedoman striker, Seaman Neal, to whom Walker had delegated responsibility for taking care of Lockwood-san.

"How's she doing?" Pierpont asked.

"All right," said Neal. "All she does is drink milk, sleep, shit, and piss."

"Not a bad life."

"How long are Mr. Hunt and them going to be on the beach?"

"Twenty-four hours," said Pierpont.

Neal shook his head. "Crazy."

"Gutsy," Pierpont said.

"I didn't think Mr. Hunt had the balls," said Neal.

Nor had Pierpont or anybody else. Hunt was a lawyer, a paperwork man, and his volunteer mission had caught them all by surprise.

The first sitting drifted off. The mess cooks cleared and wiped the tables, and the second section sat down on the benches. The mess cooks passed plates of eggs, bacon, toast, doughnuts, sweet rolls, canned fruit juice.

"When are we going to get the hell out of here?" asked Bill Gilsey, the electrician, sitting opposite Pierpont. Gilsey was abrasive, getting on Pierpont's nerves.

"Tonight," said Pierpont. "When they get back."

They felt a sudden and severe jolt. *Shark* rolled sharply to port, and the hubbub in the crew's mess died instantly. Another sharp jolt, and the boat rolled to starboard, then righted itself. They could feel a tremor through the hull, then a deep, resonant vibration.

Gilsey broke the silence. "What the fuck is that?"

The vibration continued another ten seconds, and when it stopped, they heard Mills in the control room shouting, "Get her off the bottom! Come up to periscope depth. Battle stations!"

They were on their feet, scrambling out of the crew's mess, when the alarm began bonging. When Pierpont, Jones, Weir, and the others reached the conning tower, Mills was at the periscope.

"I don't see *anything*," Mills said. "I thought it was an external explosion, but I don't see any fire or smoke."

"Captain," said Bell at the TDC, "I think it was an earthquake. They have earthquakes all the time around here."

Mills pondered this suggestion. Earthquake had been the furthest thing from his mind. After a moment he said quietly, and a bit sheepishly, "You know, Jim, I think you're right. Secure from battle stations."

# CHAPTER THIRTY-SEVEN

The earth tremor jarred Hunt, Walker, and Vogel awake.

"Keeerist," said Walker, getting fearfully to his knees. "What the hell?"

Hunt had recognized the familiar jolt at once. "Don't worry," he said. "Just a mild earthquake. Very common."

The tremor ceased as suddenly as it began.

"I thought it was the end of the world," said Vogel.

Hunt looked at the cloudless sky. Morning twilight was coming on. "Going to be a beautiful day," he said as they passed the canteen of cold coffee and shared the emergency rations. Afterward, at dawn, they slowly parted the grass and surveyed the base. There was little activity now. Hunt counted thirteen I-boats moored at the finger piers. Each had a deck watch topside, but otherwise there was no sign of life.

Focusing his binoculars on the nearest I-boat, Hunt saw something strange on the bow, aft of the capstan. It appeared to be a steel cradle. In fact, there were two cradles side by side. Farther aft, just forward of the conning tower, he saw two more cradles, and sweeping his binoculars down the piers, he saw that every I-boat had four cradles on its bow.

Walker had been likewise examining the boats. He said to Hunt, "You see what I see?"

"The cradles?"

"Yes," Walker said. "That's what they're doing here—welding those cradles on."

"But what goes in the cradles?" said Hunt.

"Your guess is as good as mine."

# CHAPTER THIRTY-EIGHT

Al Weir found Doc Jones in the crew's mess playing cribbage with Nutting. When Jones pegged out to win, Weir said with unusual politeness, "May I see you privately, Doc?"

Jones looked at Weir with utter contempt. He had never really disliked anyone in his life, but he had grown to despise the sight of Al Weir.

By regulation, Jones could not refuse a consultation. He got up and followed Weir to an empty corner of the mess. "What is it now, Weir?"

"Sorry to bother you," Weir said almost unctuously. "I need a hot-water bottle and a light-duty slip."

"A wh—what?" Jones sputtered. "What's the matter with you?"

"Phlebitis," Weir said gravely. "Thrombophlebitis."

Jones stared at Weir openmouthed. "Where's the phlebitis?" he asked.

"In my left leg. My foot is swollen and I have a pain and a tingling sensation in the fleshy part of my calf." He reached down and pulled up his trouser leg.

Jones didn't look at the leg. His face was tight, his throat dry. He was losing control to a blind rage. "Why the fuck did you volunteer for submarine duty?" he shouted, his face going red.

"For the extra pay," Weir said. "What business is that of yours?"

"You don't belong in submarines!" Jones screamed. "You're a fucking psycho! I don't give a shit whether you're an electronic genius or not. When we get in, I'm going to disqualify you from submarine duty—if I have to go all the way to the admiral!"

"Don't call me a fucking psycho, you fucking quack," Weir exploded, clenching his fists.

Jones lost control and swung at Weir with everything he had. He missed, the thrust of his swing threw him off-balance, and he crashed to the deck. In a flash, Nutting was on his feet, bending over, helping Jones get up.

"Knock this off!" a commanding voice boomed. It was Pops Wheeler coming from the control room. "What's going on?"

"He swung at me," said Weir. "After first depriving me of medical assistance."

"What the hell's wrong with you now?" Wheeler said.

"Phlebitis," Weir said, drawing himself up.

"What?"

"A blood clot in my leg."

"Well, Jesus H. Christ," Wheeler said in total exasperation, his anger causing a shortness of breath.

Jones had calmed down, and he said, "There's nothing wrong with him. He's a fuck-off artist. He wants a light-duty slip."

"My ass!" Wheeler said.

"Then I want to see the captain," Weir said.

"The captain's sleeping," said Wheeler.

"I want to file charges," Weir said.

"One more word out of you," Wheeler said, tapping Weir on the chest, "and you go on report."

# CHAPTER THIRTY-NINE

For six hours, Hunt, Walker, and Vogel lay in the grass observing the activity on the base. Hunt made copious notes on all they saw, but he knew it was merely make-work. They still didn't know what was supposed to go in those cradles. No one had even suggested a reasonable possibility. Only eight hours remained before the rendezvous with *Shark,* and they hadn't accomplished anything noteworthy.

At 1236, they heard the shrill toot of a railway locomotive as a chunky yard engine came around the bend on the dockside tracks. It was towing two flatcars, and on each car was something long and cylindrical that was covered by a tarp. Several guards with carbines sat atop the tarps. The engine moved along slowly and stopped at the finger piers.

A Japanese officer hurried out of the door of one of the barrackslike structures and walked purposefully over to the engine. The engineer climbed out of the cab with a sheaf of papers and handed them to the officer, who flipped through the pages, signing his name several times. Navies were the same worldwide, Hunt thought. Sign in quadruplicate.

The enginer uncoupled the engine from the flatcar, returned to his cab, and the engine moved off, leaving the two flatcars and the guards. Six other Japanese naval officers came from the building, talking and gesticulating. They joined the first officer, who was in the process of ordering the guards off the cars. From all appearances, Hunt judged, the cargo on the flatcars had long been expected and was now causing intense excitement among the officers, who began untying the tarps.

"Jesus H. Christ!" Vogel exclaimed. "Look at *that!*"

Hunt was holding his breath, his mind swimming. On the flatcar was a gigantic torpedo—at least fifty feet long and four or five feet in diameter—more than twice the size of an ordinary submarine torpedo.

"*That's* what goes in the cradles," Walker said.

"But how the hell do they fire them?" said Vogel. "You can't fire a torpedo without a torpedo tube."

Hunt focused his binoculars on one of the buildings where two or three dozen enthusiastic young officers came bursting out of the door and lined up in formation on the dock. They wore khaki uniforms, black boots, and Sam Browne belts with swords, and each had a white ceremonial sash tied around his head.

A portly senior naval officer came out, saluted the Imperial Navy flag, turned toward Tokyo, and bowed. The younger officers also pivoted and bowed.

"Bowing to the emperor," Hunt said.

The young men burst into song, and the observers could hear the sound clearly. It was "Kimigayo," the Japanese national anthem, Hunt told them.

At the conclusion of the anthem, the senior officer barked orders, and four of the young officers fell out of ranks and walked smartly toward the flatcar. As they approached, the guards held their rifles at "present arms," and the officers saluted. Then all four climbed atop the torpedo.

Hunt glued his binoculars on the four officers, one of whom knelt and opened a large circular submarine-type hatch midway along the top of the torpedo. He climbed inside the torpedo, closing the hatch behind him, and moments later, a tiny periscope arose from the top of the torpedo near the hatch.

Hunt held his breath in astonishment. Everything suddenly fell into place.

"A human torpedo!" Walker was first to use the chilling phrase.

"That's what it is," said Hunt. "Those young officers with the white headbands are a *Tokko* group—a suicide corps."

"I'll bet that's what got *Florida* and *Osage!*" said Vogel. "An I-boat couldn't have gotten through the nets at Majuro and Eniwetok, but it could have launched those babies. They'd go right through the net."

"Exactly," said Hunt, feeling a tremendous sense of achievement at their discovery. Suicide corps! So Japan had been driven to that extreme. Dozens of young men inflamed with the mysticism of Shinto, sacrificing themselves for the emperor so they would obtain glory in the next world. This could be a disastrous threat to the American Pacific Fleet. If each torpedo pilot struck one capital ship—a carrier or a battleship —the losses would be staggering, perhaps decisive.

When the hatch on the torpedo opened, and the officer climbed out, another officer descended and closed the hatch. They must have spent weeks in a classroom with models and mock-ups, thought Hunt. Now they were getting the feel of the real thing. He took out a note pad and made a sketch of the torpedo. His report would shake the U.S. Navy to its foundation. They must be thorough—and they must get back.

# CHAPTER FORTY

At a table in the mess hall, Jack Childress sat sketching the low-pressure blower system into his qualification notebook. The compartment was noisy, jammed with off-duty personnel playing acey-deucey and cribbage.

Mills came into the compartment from control. He was wearing his red baseball cap, and he had a big cigar jutting from his mouth. The men fell silent. A few, including Childress, started to rise.

"At ease, men," Mills boomed. He grinned, slapped the baker, Johnny Webster, on his back, and walked over to look at the cribbage tournament ladder on the bulletin board. "Where's Willie the Silent?" he said.

"In the sack, captain," Doc Jones said. Jones was playing cribbage with Red Weaver.

"He's my next opponent," said Mills. "Tell him the Old Man is hot out for his ass."

"I'll get him, captain," said Tom Dunlop, the fireman.

Dunlop returned a moment later, leading a sleepy-eyed Willie Bonsel. Willie nodded silently to the captain and drew a mug of coffee. The men gave way. Mills and Bonsel sat down at a table, and while Bonsel sipped his coffee and tried his best to look alert, Mills idly shuffled and dealt the cards. The men gathered around to watch what was certain to be a perfect slaughter.

From his seat in a far corner, Jack Childress appraised the Old Man. Mills had thrown himself into the game, seemingly oblivious to the fact that

*Shark* lay in seventy-two feet of water a mile and a quarter off Yokosuka Naval Base, where even now (Childress thought with a shudder) Mr. Hunt and Walker and Vogel might be undergoing torture or getting injected with truth serum to reveal how they got ashore. There was no question in Childress's mind: Mills had been cast from a very special mold. A remarkable man, apparently without fear.

A voice on the PA system rang out: "*Captain to the conning tower. Captain to the conning tower.*"

Mills jumped up and raced to control, then up the ladder to the conning tower.

Wally Yates had the deck. "Captain," he said, "we can hear somebody pinging out there."

"Pinging?" said Mills. "Why? Where?" He paused to listen, and then he heard the faint metallic echo.

Mills ordered the boat off the bottom and the sound heads rigged out. He summoned Doc Jones to man the sonar.

Jones reported and manned the gear, and a moment later he said, "Slow, light screws zero-nine-zero true. I'd say it was a patrol boat."

"Give me a few inches of periscope," said Mills, kneeling on the deck to grab the handles. "Sixty-five feet. Put me on zero-nine-zero."

Wally Yates handled the scope. Mills exposed only three inches of the glass. He reported, "Small PC. Angle on the bow ninety starboard. Probably six thousand yards off. Down scope."

Holding the dividers, Yates bent over the chart. Then he said, "Captain, that's just about where those sampans fouled their nets on us the other day."

Mills swore under his breath. Then he looked at the chart. There was the place where Pierpont had made a small red X and labeled it *Nets*. He nodded; then he said to Yates, "How about this scenario? The fishermen report the fouling and loss of their nets to the port authorities. After all the paperwork is filed, the harbor patrol routinely investigates. They ping around out there today. They find nothing. They turn in a negative report. No need for us to worry. Right?"

"I hope so, captain," said Yates.

"Okay, Wally," said Mills. "Rig in the sound heads, secure sonar, put her back on the bottom."

"Aye, captain."

At that moment, the watch messenger stuck his head into the conning tower. "Mr. Yates? Doc is wanted on the double in the chiefs' quarters. It's Pops."

Jones barely touched the rungs going down the ladder to control. He raced forward to the crew's quarters and found Wheeler lying on the deck clutching his chest and moaning. Jones saw instantly that it was a coronary. Mills appeared in the doorway, and Jones said, "Heart attack! I need morphine and oxygen!"

Mills charged to the medical locker in the after battery, shouting along the way to the chief of the watch to rig up a Momsen lung and oxygen bottle and take it to Jones. By the time Mills got back to the chiefs' quarters with the morphine and syringe, Jones was administering oxygen, holding the Momsen lung over Pops's face.

"How is he?" Mills said anxiously, kneeling.

"Bad! It's a bad one," Jones said as he injected the morphine into Wheeler's tattooed arm. "That will relieve the pain and ease the shock," he said to Mills. "Let's get him into his bunk."

They lifted Wheeler's huge bulk into his bunk, and while Mills held the Momsen lung to his face, Jones opened his shirt and listened to his heart with a stethoscope.

After a time, Jones said, "He's got to have absolute rest, captain. You'll have to relieve him and name a new chief of the boat."

"Poor guy. It's the end of the road for him."

"If he lives, they'll survey him out," Jones said.

"*If* he lives?" Mills echoed.

"He might have another one," said Jones. "I'll put him on phenobarbital to keep him relaxed, but in these situations anything can happen. He should be hospitalized as soon as possible."

"Yes," said Mills, "of course."

Mills returned to his cabin, stunned and bewildered. Heart attack! He'd never heard of a sailor having a heart attack. Only admirals, commodores, and very senior captains had heart attacks. He sat at his desk and scratched out a bulletin board notice for Weaver to type:

ALL HANDS.
*Effective immediately, Chief Quartermaster Robert L. Pierpont will become Acting Chief of the Boat.*

Pierpont was next in line in terms of seniority. It was a long-overdue promotion.

The word about Pops Wheeler spread through the boat like a strong wind. The crew was shocked dumb.

Carl Corley expressed the view of a small—but growing—minority: "It's having that fucking female on board. I tell you, the boat's jinxed."

## CHAPTER FORTY-ONE

In the fading afternoon light, as Tony Walker covered the right sector of the base with his binoculars, he saw a large crane coming around the corner of a concrete building.

"Look at that," he said.

The crane moved along a set of railway tracks adjacent to the human-torpedo flatcars. It stopped next to the forward car, and presently a truck came onto the dock loaded with workmen.

"They're going to put those torpedoes on a boat," Walker said, guessing aloud. "That boat right there. Here come a couple of officers from the boat."

Hunt saw that one of these men was equivalent in rank to a lieutenant commander. He said, "The skipper and exec, I'll bet."

"Here comes Fatso," said Vogel, who was covering the left sector. It was the nickname they had bestowed on the portly senior naval officer. They had concluded earlier that he was the commanding officer of the human-torpedo school.

They watched a conference taking place between Fatso, the sub's skipper, the exec, the foreman of the workers, and the crane operator. Fatso pointed to the crane and the I-boat, apparently giving detailed instructions, and then the meeting broke up amid gales of laughter.

Walker was right. The workmen rigged a big sling beneath the torpedo, plus a slew of guidelines. The crane hook was inserted into the hook on the sling, and the crane slowly lifted the torpedo from the cradle on the flatcar while the workmen kept a strain on the guidelines to keep the torpedo from swinging. Fatso waddled here and there, giving hand signals to the crane operator, and after a time the torpedo nestled into the two port cradles on the I-boat. The skipper and exec watched pensively from the I-boat's bridge. Hunt wondered what they thought about their new weapons system.

"My God," said Walker, awestruck. The torpedo occupied almost the whole of the forward port deck, and the I-boat itself settled another foot deeper in the water.

As Hunt, Walker, and Vogel watched in silence, the crane lifted the other torpedo off the flatcar, gently lowered it into the starboard cradles, and the workmen came aboard and secured the torpedoes with heavy rigging. Hunt made detailed sketches of the securing gear.

Several minutes later, the amidships hatch on the port torpedo opened, and one of the young torpedo "pilots" (as the three had dubbed them) came up and sat on the torpedo.

"Where did he come from?" said Walker. "He wasn't inside when the crane lifted it."

"There must be an access hatch from inside the submarine," said Vogel.

"Yeah," said Walker. "There'd have to be. The air supply inside that torpedo must be limited. Several hours at most."

Hunt jotted down these speculations, glad now that Mills had insisted he take two men along. Not only were they technically excellent, they were also good company. Without them, it would be very lonely on the cliff. He tucked his folded notes and sketches into his shirt pocket with a feeling of immense satisfaction. There was a lot more he wanted to know about the suicide weapon—such as power plant, speed, range, size of warhead—but, from the information he would provide, such data could be extrapolated fairly accurately by experts. The important thing was the discovery of the system itself, for the mere knowledge of its existence would enable the U.S. Navy to take effective countermeasures.

He looked at his watch: 1700. Sunset in one hour. A half hour after that, at 1830, they would leave. That would give them an hour and a half to reach the rendezvous with *Shark*.

# CHAPTER FORTY-TWO

Al Weir lay in his bunk in the darkened crew's sleeping quarters. He had a flashlight propped over his left shoulder, and it shone on the pages of the book he was reading: *The Farmer's Almanac Home Medical Adviser.* He was deeply absorbed in the section on ulcers.

Touring the boat in his new capacity as chief of the boat, Bob Pierpont entered the compartment from the crew's mess hall. He was mending some political fences, showing his flag, hearing some new beefs the men had been loath to load on Pops Wheeler, and laying down some new policy of his own. He was deeply fond of Pops, and he was not at all happy about how he had acquired his new status—but he was damned glad to have it.

He noticed the light and made his way toward it. He knew it came from Weir's bunk. No one else spent time in the sack reading.

Pierpont knelt and said, "Whatcha reading, Al?" and Weir hastily snapped off the flashlight and laid the book aside. A sixth sense told Pierpont that something was amiss, and he reached for the book. Weir grabbed his hand.

"Let me see that book," Pierpont demanded icily.

"It's none of your goddamned business," Weir said through gritted teeth.

"Everything on this boat's my business now," said Pierpont. He tore Weir's hand away, grabbed the book, and snapped on the flashlight.

"Well I'll be damned," said Pierpont. "You fuck-off artist! So this is where you get your poop!" he tossed the flashlight on the bunk and stalked off, heading for the captain's cabin, where he gave the book to Mills. "I recommend that you confiscate this book for the rest of the patrol, captain."

Mills leafed through the book and returned it to Pierpont. "Show it to Doc and tell him to lock it up in the medical locker," he said.

"Aye, aye."

"We'll get rid of Weirdo Weir when we get in," Mills said, "but meantime, we need him badly. Handle him with the proverbial gloved fist, Bob."

"Aye, aye, sir," Pierpont said, turning to leave.

"Oh, Bob—"

"Yes, sir?"

"Nice work."

The two old shipmates exchanged grins.

"Captain," said Pierpont, suddenly serious, "as chief of the boat, I strongly recommend you get a couple hours' shut-eye."

"Aye, aye," said Mills. "I'll give it a try."

## CHAPTER FORTY-THREE

At 1800, the watch messenger knocked on Mills's bulkhead to report sunset. Mills snapped awake straight out of a nightmare. He fumbled to his sink, washed his face, and stared into the mirror. He looked like he had aged ten years, but he was clear headed and somewhat elated. In two hours, whether the mystery had been solved or not, they would pick up the shore party and get the hell out of Tokyo Bay. They had done their best to discharge their orders to "reconnoiter Yokosuka Naval Base," and to remain any longer would unduly risk the boat and the lives of the officers and crew.

He stepped across the passageway to the chiefs' quarters where Pops Wheeler was propped up on a nest of pillows and Doc Jones was spoon-feeding him broth.

Wheeler smiled wanly. "I hear you busted me, captain."

Mills forced a laugh. "Only temporarily, Pops. You'll be back on your feet in no time. By the way, you better get your ass on a diet."

Tears filmed over Wheeler's eyes. "Why bother, captain?" he said. "It's all over for me. I'm walking athwartships."

"They'll give you a nice cushy desk job Stateside," Mills said.

"Not with a bum ticker," said Wheeler, tapping his chest. "They'll give me a medical survey board, that's what they'll give me. I won't make twenty years."

"We'll see about that," Mills said. "It's a combat-incurred disability. Anyway, stop worrying about it. In two hours we'll be pulling out of here. Now take it easy."

"Yeah," Jones echoed. "Take it easy, goddamn it."

Going aft, Mills paused at the door of the yeoman's shack, an ingeniously engineered space, not much larger than a telephone booth. Red Weaver sat at his typewriter trying to cope with a mountain of paperwork.

"Hello, Red," said Mills, placing a friendly hand on his shoulder.

"Oh, hello, captain." Weaver swiveled around in his chair. "I've started on the transfers today. Should be done in a couple of days."

"You yeomen have had it too easy for too long," Mills joshed. "Now you're going to earn your pay."

"I'll say, sir," Weaver returned. "Pierpont put out the word to get all recommended promotions in by next Friday. He figures you—"

"Is this what they call a broad hint?" Mills broke in, grinning.

Red Weaver blushed for the first time in his life. He stammered, "Well, sir, er, ah, I've got all my courses in, passed the test, have the time in grade—"

"You don't strike me as chief petty officer material," Mills said gravely. "I heard you think there's a Jap bullet with your name on it out there somewhere. How can I promote a *Shark* sailor with a negative attitude like that?"

Red Weaver paled. "Who told you that, sir?"

"A little birdie," Mills said, again grinning. "But don't worry, Red. We'll have you out of here in two—three hours. You won't have to worry about that bullet anymore."

"Aye, aye, sir," said Weaver. Inwardly he quivered. He was one of the most supersititous men alive.

In the control room, Mills paused for a jovial moment with the men on watch. One of these was the lookout, Seaman Neal, now manning the idle stern plane wheel.

"How's Lockwood-san getting on?" Mills asked.

"Just fine, sir," Neal said. "Well—actually, she's been crying a lot today. Doc says she has, er, some kind of upset tummy."

"Colic?" Mills asked.

"Yes, sir. That's it! Colic."

"Well, don't worry, Neal," Mills said. "We'll have Mother Walker back in a couple of hours."

"Yes, sir," Neal said, beaming. "I'll certainly be glad to see him."

"You and me both," said Mills as he climbed up the conning-tower ladder.

In the conning tower, Mills glanced at the clock: 1810. He said to the OOD, "Periscope depth, please." The joviality was gone. Mills was concentrating completely on the task at hand—and the perils that lay beyond. It was no time to fumble the ball.

## CHAPTER FORTY-FOUR

Hunt glanced at his wristwatch and said, "Let's go." It was dark and clear, with no moon. They moved uphill through the thick grass and trees to the edge of the clearing where the antiaircraft battery was encamped. They paused a moment at the edge of the clearing, waiting for the patrolling sentry to walk around the corner, out of sight.

"Okay," Hunt said, raising his hand, and they moved on in a half crouch, just inside the edge of the thicket. Hunt felt naked. He wished they had the protection of last night's rain.

When they were halfway around the grassy clearing, Hunt's foot landed hard on an old limb that snapped with a piercing crack. All three men froze, hearts pounding, watching the compound. A large German shepherd raced from the sandbags toward them, barking viciously as Vogel unslung his submachine gun and Walker pulled a knife from its sheath.

At that instant, floodlights blazed on, turning the clearing from night to day. The dog reached them, barking, lunging, drawing back, lunging. The sentry appeared around the corner, saw them, and shouted in Japanese, "Halt!"

Hunt shouted back in Japanese, "Call your stupid dog!"

"Who goes there?" the sentry shouted, running

toward them, unslinging his rifle. He was the tallest Jap Hunt had ever seen.

"Lieutenant Orita," Hunt called out, "and a party of two enlisted men. Call off your dog."

The sentry shouted at the dog, then leveled his rifle on them. They could see other soldiers coming out of the compound to see what was going on. They had no further options.

Hunt said softly, "Let him have it, Vogel," and Vogel skillfully cut the sentry down with one brief burst.

"Run for the cliff!" shouted Hunt.

They plunged into the thicket, running at full speed. Behind them, they heard loud shouting and then a siren, and two or three minutes later they heard sirens going off all over the base. They crossed the gravel road at full tilt, reentered the thicket, and stopped to listen. They could hear more shouting behind them, a search party organizing.

"Come on," said Hunt, pulling out his pistol. "Let's go."

They ran and stumbled, crashing through the thicket. The downhill slope was steeper now, and they were half falling toward the cliff face. Vogel tripped on a root, pitched forward, and hit the ground with a heavy thud. He cried out in pain, "My ankle!"

Hunt and Walker turned back and lifted Vogel to his feet. He couldn't stand on the ankle.

"Do your best," Hunt said to Vogel. "It's not much farther."

They pushed on, Hunt and Walker half lifting Vogel from the ground. The pain was blinding. He couldn't help moaning, and finally he said, "Leave me! I can't stand it."

"No, no," said Hunt. "Come on." He picked up a stick. "Bite hard on this."

They reached the top of the cliff. The ledge at its foot seemed a mile down. Hunt anchored the coiled rope and let the bitter end fall. It dangled ten feet above the ledge. They would have to drop that distance.

"You first," Hunt said to Walker. "Inflate the boat."

"Aye, aye," said Walker. He grabbed the rope and went down the cliff like a monkey, dropping the last ten feet.

"Now you," Hunt said to Vogel.

Vogel looked doubtful.

"Hurry," said Hunt. "Give me your Thompson."

Vogel handed over the submachine gun and started down the rope, still biting hard on the stick and sweating with pain. Near the end of the rope, he found a handhold and attempted to crawl backward down the last ten feet. But he slipped and fell—with a heavy thud and a scream of pain.

Hunt could hear people crashing through the thicket, then shouting, very close. Two or three soldiers, he estimated. His heart pounding, he cocked his gun. Better to take care of things here, for he and Walker and Vogel would be completely exposed on the ledge below. He waited for the next shout, only five or ten feet away, then he pulled the trigger, holding the barrel level, spraying the thicket back and forth. He heard two cries of pain. Then the gun was empty. He tossed it aside and slid down the rope, searing the palms of his hands.

Walker was launching the dinghy; Vogel was propped against the cliff, biting on the stick. His face was contorted with pain, his eyes watery.

"I got two of them, I think," Hunt said to Walker.

A carbine burst overhead, and the whining bullets ricocheted against the rocks.

"Keeerist," Walker cried, grabbing his Thompson. He aimed it straight up the cliff and let off a brief burst. A soldier cried out, pitched off the cliff, and fell to the rocks not more than ten feet away. Walker stared up the cliff a moment, amazed at his markmanship.

They helped Vogel into the dinghy, then climbed in behind him, and Walker manned the oars, rowing furiously out into the dark waters.

# CHAPTER FORTY-FIVE

At 1945, Mills said quietly, "Surface."

*Shark* came to the surface near the breakwater, and Mills hurried to the dripping bridge. He swept his binoculars toward the island, but he could see no sign of the shore party.

"Four main engines on the battery charge," Mills said into the intercom. "Propulsion on the dinky." The batteries were low.

He heard the main induction clank open and then the throaty roar of the four diesels.

"Right full rudder," Mills said. "Dead slow ahead." He would circle until they arrived.

He focused his binoculars on the base, examining it closely. There appeared to be far more activity than they had observed before. Vehicles darting to and fro, men running all over the place as though—Mills thought with a sinking feeling—responding to an alarm. A movement near the finger piers caught his eye, and he could now make out two PT-like boats pulling away from the finger piers, moving fast toward the dark blot of the island. Moments later, both boats snapped on powerful bridge searchlights which probed the water ahead. With mounting dread, Mills watched the two craft. They were headed directly toward the track the rubber dinghy would have to take.

"Secure the battery charge!" he shouted at the intercom. "Put all four main engines on the line. Come left to two-four-zero. Battle stations surface!" he pulled the bridge battle alarm.

The gun crew poured out on deck from the gun access hatch. It was missing its leader, Tony Walker, but Walker's assistant took over, and soon the gun was manned and ready, the ammo passers in place. Other men manned the 40 mm on the cigarette deck.

Mills turned to Jack Childress. "Where's Pierpont?"

"Sir, he's in the control room on the blow-and vent manifold," said Childress.

"Oh," said Mills. He had forgotten that Pierpont was now chief of the boat. Control was his proper battle station, and Childress had been appointed to replace him on the bridge.

"All ahead emergency," Mills said, his eyes glued in the TBT, which was now fixed on the two PT boats.

Childress could scarcely believe what he saw. He figured the Old Man had taken leave of his senses. They were charging the base like a troop of cavalry. He had never felt such fear.

"Radar, do you have those PT boats dead ahead?" Mills said coolly.

"Range one-oh-oh-oh," Weir said. One-half mile.

Mills shouted the range to the gun crew, who had trained the gun on the searchlights. Then he said to Childress, "Keep a watch for the dinghy."

"Aye, aye," said Childress, happy to have something specific to do.

"Range eight-oh-oh," Weir said. "Closing fast."

"Very well," Mills said, and once again he relayed the range to the gun crew.

As he had been taught, Childress kept his binoculars two degrees above the horizon as he swept the water. He blinked, looked hard again, and saw the dinghy dead ahead. "Dinghy! Zero-zero-zero, relative," he cried.

Mills swung his binoculars until he located the dinghy, about halfway between *Shark* and the PT boats.

"Left full rudder!" he said to the intercom. "Ahead two-thirds."

*Shark* swung to the left, and then Childress realized what Mills intended to do: he was going to put *Shark* between the PT boats and the dinghy. Childress kept his binoculars on the dinghy, which was now drawing to starboard.

"Right full rudder," Mills said, "all ahead one-third," and *Shark* swung right, slowing abruptly.

# CHAPTER FORTY-SIX

Tony Walker pulled on the oars, head down, gasping.

As Hunt shifted his binoculars from the PT boats to the onrushing *Shark*, he understood what Mills had done. *Shark* now lay between the PT boats and the dinghy. It was the most beautiful piece of seamanship Hunt had ever seen.

"Reverse course!" he shouted to Walker.

"What?" said Walker, too busy rowing to see what had happened.

"Come about," Hunt said. "*Shark's* behind us."

Walker spun the dinghy on its axis and rowed desperately.

"Less than a hundred yards," Hunt said, looking through his binoculars. He could see *Shark's* deck gun, manned and trained on the oncoming PT boats, which had obviously not seen *Shark*.

"Range five-oh-oh," Weir said.

"Stand by the main battery," Mills shouted at the gun crew. "Range five hundred yards."

The PT boats, their searchlights sweeping the water, were coming on very slowly, still unaware of *Shark*.

"Where's the dinghy?" said Mills, his binoculars on the PT boats.

"Fifty yards off the starboard beam, captain," Childress said. It seemed to him like fifty miles.

Mills shouted at the gun crew, "Two men stand by to recover the dinghy on the starboard side."

"Forty yards," Childress reported. Hurry. Hurry. Hurry.

One of the two seachlights from the PT boats abruptly tilted skyward, then leveled on *Shark*. It was a blinding, terrifying light.

"Fire!" Mills cried out.

The main deck gun opened up instantly, and then the 40 mm commenced firing, tracers sweeping toward the searchlights.

The third round from the main gun hit the first PT boat directly amidships. It blew up and sank instantly, a mass of smoke and flames.

"Dinghy's here!" Childress shouted, looking down as two of the gun crew pulled Hunt, Walker, and Vogel up the saddle tanks onto the deck. "They're aboard, sir."

"Very well," Mills shouted above the roar of gunfire. "Right full rudder. All ahead emergency."

As Hunt and Walker helped Vogel to the bridge, Vogel was still biting on the stick.

"Get below!" Mills yelled to the shore party, and Hunt and Walker lowered Vogel down the hatch, shouting for assistance.

The second PT boat pulled away, zigzagging

at high speed, its searchlight off. Mills watched it, swearing aloud. He would have liked to have bagged it, too, but now that would be impossible.

"Secure the guns," he called. "Gun crews below."

The guns were quickly secured, and the men went belowdecks.

Hunt returned to the bridge where he found Mills coolly directing *Shark* away from the base at maximum speed.

"Thanks for the rescue, captain," said Hunt.

"What happened?" Mills asked him.

"They discovered us, and we had to run for it. We had a fire fight. No injuries other than Vogel, who sprained his ankle. I imagine by now the whole Jap navy is on alert."

"You can bet on that," Mills said. "Did you find out anything?"

"Everything," said Hunt.

Barreling along at 20.6 knots toward the deeper, open water of Tokyo Bay, *Shark* left the breakwater on the port quarter.

"Aircraft," Weir reported. "Four, five planes. Range ten miles."

"Here they come," said Mills. "Take a sounding."

A moment later, Pierpont reported from control. "Thirty fathoms, captain."

"Clear the bridge," Mills ordered. "Dive! Dive!"

# CHAPTER FORTY-SEVEN

*Shark* leveled off at 150 feet, and every man in the conning tower fixed his eyes on Mills. Bill

Gilsey stuck his head up the conning-tower hatch and said, "Hate to bother you like this, captain, but we've got to have a battery charge."

"Yes," Mills said, deep in thought, "I know."

"High-speed screws at zero-four-zero," Doc Jones reported.

"Very well," said Mills, still preoccupied. Suddenly he turned to Hunt. "There's a way to cripple that Jap suicide corps. We've got twenty-six torpedoes. Those moored I-boats are sitting ducks. We could probably sink one with each fish."

Hunt pondered this typically Mauler Mills suggestion, thinking, the best defense is a strong offense. He replied carefully. "I think we could get one or two, maybe three, but they'd nail us before we got four, and that wouldn't cripple the program. Captain, I think it's more important to get out of here and take the news back."

"High-speed screws all around the dial," Jones reported.

"Very well," Mills said. "Rig for silent running." Then to Hunt: "They're sealing us off. We have no battery. We can't maneuver. How do you propose we get out?"

"By doing the unexpected," said Hunt.

"And what might *that* be, Mr. Hunt?"

"Captain, they'll assume that we'll try to run for the net, and they'll try to cut us off. What if we did the opposite? What if we ran into the anchorage, surfaced among the I-boats, lay to, and charged our batteries? I think we look enough like an I-boat to get away with it. After we have the charge, we can figure out what to do."

Mills thought about that. It certainly would be an unexpected maneuver, and it might work. And they *had* to have a battery charge.

"Pinging," Jones said. "Short-scale. I think he's got us."

"All right, Mr. Hunt," Mills said quietly. "Give me a course to the anchorage."

"Two-five-zero," Hunt said immediately.

"Come right to two-five-zero," Mills said. "All ahead full."

"I think he's making his run," Jones said.

"Very well," said Mills. "Rig for depth charge." The telephone talker passed the word.

"Here he comes!" Jones said. They could hear the screws through the hull.

"Left full rudder," said Mills. "All stop."

"Dropping," Jones said, removing his earphones.

The explosions were to the starboard and above and very close. WHAM! WHAM! WHAM! WHAM! WHAM! WHAM! *Shark* reeled to port. The cork insulation flew off the bulkhead, leaving motes of dust in the air. The lights flickered, then held.

"Counted six," Childress said in a wavering high-pitched voice, noting the figure in the log with trembling fingers. His ears were ringing so badly he could no longer hear clearly.

"All ahead emergency," Mills said quietly.

"He's turning around for his second run," Jones said.

"Right full rudder."

"Here he comes," said Jones, again taking off his earphones.

WHAM! WHAM! WHAM! WHAM! The explosions were closer yet, violent and deafening. They threw Mills against the radar, Childress against the chrome wheel of the helm. The lights went out and stayed out, and they turned on the emergency lamps.

"Rudder amidships," Mills said. "Radar depth. Make ready the forward tubes."

"Forward tubes ready," the telephone talker said.

"What are you going to do, captain?" Hunt asked.

"Sink the bastard," said Mills.

When *Shark* reached periscope depth, Mills

glued his eye into the eyepiece, walked the scope, and stopped. "There she is," he said. "Fleet destroyer. Angle on the bow, ten port. She's turning. Stand by. *Mark!*"

"Radar depth."

"Man the SJ," said Mills, still glued to the scope. "Give me a range and bearing."

"Bearing one-two-four, range one-two-oh-oh," Weir said.

Bell and Yates, manning the TDC, cranked in the flow of information.

"All ahead two-thirds," Mills said. "Open the outer doors on one, two, and three."

"Outer doors open, one, two, and three."

Hunt suddenly spoke up. "Captain, I don't think it's advisable to shoot at that fellow."

*"What?"* Mills said, stepping back from the periscope.

"Chances are he thinks he's already got us," said Hunt. "You know how overconfident they are about killing our boats. If you shoot and miss, they'll hear our torpedoes, they'll know we're still alive and kicking, and they'll be right on top of us again. And if you hit, everybody in Tokyo Bay will know it."

Mills took off his baseball cap and scratched his head. Then he said quietly, "Ahead one-third. Secure the approach. Close the outer doors. One hundred feet."

After a moment, Jones said, "Captain, it's raining again. Hard."

Childress sighed. Thank God! The rain would foul the destroyer's sonar.

"He's turning away, captain," Jones reported. "He's lost us."

"Let's get to that damned anchorage," said Mills. "Come right to two-five-zero."

They maneuvered toward the anchorage, planing up to periscope depth.

"Up scope," Mills said. "All stop."

He grabbed the handles and walked the scope around. "It sure is raining! Ain't we lucky? Stand by. *Mark!*"

"Zero-zero-one," Hunt said, reading the azimuth.

"That's the breakwater light," said Mills.

Childress plotted the bearing line on the chart. His fingers were steadier now.

"I-boat," said Mills. "Mark!"

"One-six-five," said Hunt.

"Surface!" said Mills.

They came up slowly, as planned, surfacing in the anchorage. Mills went to the bridge first, wearing foul weather gear. It was raining hard. He spoke into the intercom: "Charge batteries on four main engines, propulsion on the dinky."

Hunt joined him on the bridge, relieved to find that the rain muffled the sound of the engines. "There's little or no current in here, captain. She ought to hold without drifting."

"I think you're right," Mills said, manning the TBT. Then, "Stand by. Mark!"

He took bearings on the four closest I-boats, and in the conning tower, Childress plotted these on the chart. They would recheck the bearings every ten minutes to make certain they were not drifting.

Hunt put his binoculars on the closest I-boat, which was about a hundred yards away. He could barely make out its silhouette in the rainy blackness. Then he said to Mills, "It just might work."

"Yes," Mills replied thoughtfully, "it just might." He spoke into the intercom: "Secure from battle stations. Set the normal watch."

Childress stowed his gear in the chart-table drawer and went down to the control room. It was crowded with men securing from battle stations and the normal watch standers taking over. Pierpont said to Childress, "Good work up there. You all right?"

"I've never been so scared in my whole god-damn life," Childress answered.

"You ain't alone," said Pierpont.

"I'm *still* scared," said Childress. "How the hell are we going to get out of here?"

Pierpont shook his head. Truthfully, he did not know. "The Old Man'll think of something. Let's get some java."

Normal lighting and power had been restored in the crew's mess, and it was jammed and noisy there. Tokyo Rose blared swing music above the din. Suddenly the music stopped, and her dulcet voice began speaking. The men fell silent.

*"Boys, here's an Imperial Fleet news bulletin: An American submarine was sunk in shallow water tonight in Tokyo Bay near the Yokosuka Naval Base. The officers and crew were drowned. That is the seventy-ninth confirmed sinking of an American submarine by the glorious and intrepid men of the Imperial Fleet this year. Now all you boys in American submarines on patrol, mourn your lost shipmates and reconsider. Wouldn't you rather be home with your loved ones than out there facing certain death on the high seas?"*

"You bet your sweet ass I would," Red Weaver said loudly toward the radio. The men broke up with laughter, hoots, and jeers as Tokyo Rose played "Sentimental Journey"—the song she always played after announcing a submarine loss.

# CHAPTER FORTY-EIGHT

After he finished his coffee, Pierpont went forward to the chiefs' quarters. Pops Wheeler was propped up in his bunk, reading *Untamed Ecstacy,* a loan from the captain.

"How you making it?" Pierpont said.

"All right," Wheeler said. "It's tough being benched, Bob. Real tough. You have too much time to think. But I hear you did a good job."

"Not like old Pops," Pierpont said cheerily, taking off his shirt and climbing into his bunk. "Nobody can really fill your shoes."

"What happens next?" Wheeler said.

"I don't have the slightest idea," said Pierpont. "And I don't think the Old Man does, either."

"Can we get out?"

"No," Pierpont said after a long pause. "We'll try like hell, but I don't see a way out of here, Pops. I think this is finally the end of the road."

They fell silent. After a time, Wheeler said, "That Hunt's quite a guy, isn't he?"

"Amazing," said Pierpont. "Absolutely amazing. Looking at him, you'd think he was the last man on earth you'd want to go into battle with. But he'd make a hell of a skipper. Far better than Mr. Reynolds."

"Yes," said Wheeler. "Lot of brains, too. Too bad."

"Yeah," said Pierpont. "You know, Pops, I always had the feeling we'd get through."

"So did I," said Wheeler. "You expect the

other guys to get it, but I never thought we would."

"No."

Mills came into the compartment, a cigar clamped between his teeth. He stared at the two old shipmates. "You guys look like you're on your way to a funeral."

"I think we are, captain," Pierpont said. "Ours."

Mills sat down, took the cigar from his mouth, and said, "We've got them beat now. Tokyo Rose just announced that we've been sunk."

"So we heard," Pierpont said.

"They'll let down their guard," said Mills. "Then we'll make our move." He turned to Wheeler. "How you doing, Pops?"

"All right, captain," said Wheeler, grinning, "for an old man."

"We missed you," Mills said, "but Bob here did a fine job. Fine crew. Best damn crew in the whole navy." He paused. "Don't you worry about it. I'll get you home. You'll become famous. The first coronary patient ever to be depth-charged."

"In Tokyo Bay," Wheeler added.

The watch messenger knocked on the bulkhead. "Captain to the bridge."

Mills was up and off in a flash.

## CHAPTER FORTY-NINE

Topside, it was still raining hard. Jim Bell had the watch. "Captain," he said, "there's a small harbor patrol boat out there, and its going from boat to boat."

"How's the battery charge going?" said Mills,

adjusting his binoculars. He saw the patrol boat faintly as it pulled up alongside a moored I-boat.

"Half finished," said Bell.

"Mmmmmm," said Mills, nodding. Then to the intercom: "Ask Mr. Hunt to come to the bridge."

"Aye."

Mills turned to Jack Childress. "You're still wet behind the ears, Childress, but you're going to be a fine submarine sailor."

Childress was floored. "Thank—thank you, captain," he stammered, thinking, but for how long?

Hunt came on the bridge dressed in foul weather gear, and Mills briefed him on the patrol boat. Hunt examined the boat, now lying to alongside the I-boat. "He's talking to the deck watch," said Hunt.

"He's coming this way!" said Bell, his eyes in his binoculars.

Mills spoke quietly into the intercom: "Boarding party to the conning tower." Then, "Quartermaster and lookouts below."

Childress and the three lookouts ducked down the hatch.

"Captain," said Hunt, "I'll handle this. In Japanese."

"Oh!" Mills started, remembering. "You think you can?"

"Like a native," said Hunt. "Keep everybody out of sight."

Tony Walker stuck his head up the hatch. "Boarding party in the conning tower. Nelson replacing Vogel."

"Very well," Mills said. "Stand by with weapons ready."

Mills and Bell watched the oncoming boat a moment longer, then ducked below the fairwater. Only Hunt was left in sight on the bridge. The boat eased alongside smartly, lying to about ten feet abeam *Shark*'s bridge.

A man appeared on the small bridge of the boat and called out, "On board the submarine!"

"What is it?" Hunt responded in Japanese.

"All's well?"

"All but the weather," Hunt said. "Is the alert over?"

"No. The alert's still in force."

"We're wasting a lot of precious oil running our engines," Hunt said. "What's it all about anyway?"

"They say there was an American submarine inside the harbor."

Hunt laughed aloud. "Impossible!"

"I agree," the Japanese said, "but they claim they found it and sank it."

"Impossible," Hunt repeated.

"The harbor command is still very nervous," the Japanese said, "so keep a sharp eye out. Report anything unusual."

"Don't worry," Hunt said. "We will."

# CHAPTER FIFTY

Doc Jones took his ease in the forward torpedo room, chatting with Don Nutting, the duty torpedoman. Like everyone else in the crew they were assessing *Shark's* chances of escaping from Tokyo Bay. Nutting was a notorious optimist, but Doc Jones had concluded, like Pierpont, that *Shark* had reached the end of the line.

The telephone barked, interrupting their chat. Nutting answered, saying, "Yeah. He's here," and he handed the telephone to Jones.

It was Red Weaver in the crew's mess. "Doc? Can you get back here right away? It's Al Weir."

"Weir!" Jones said. "What does he think is wrong with him now?"

"He fell down the battery well," Weaver said. "He's badly hurt."

Jones slammed the phone onto its cradle, saying, "Shit!"

Passing through the forward battery passageway, Doc stepped around the well in the deck that was always left open during the battery charge. Weir had fallen into a similar hatch in the after battery deck. What a stupid accident! Even the greenest hands were aware that these hatches were open during the battery charge, and no one had ever fallen in.

Jones reached the mess hall and found Weir laid out on a table, clutching his right thigh, moaning, "My leg! My leg!" Weaver, Lyman, Webster, and the two duty messcooks were trying to minister to him.

"What's the matter with your leg?" Jones said, looking down at the man he despised.

"Broken," Weir said.

"We'll see about that," said Jones. "Freddie, get me a sharp knife."

Lyman produced the knife at once, and Jones skillfully slit the dungaree trouser on Weir's right leg and peeled it away. Then he stared, wide-eyed. The fibula was indeed broken, projecting against the skin.

"I'll be damned," said Jones. Then to Weir, "Okay, you're right. It's broken. Lie still. I'll be right back."

He got morphine and splints from the medical locker, gave Weir a shot of morphine, did the best he could (lacking X-ray equipment) to reset the bone, and tied the splints in place. He felt compassion for Weir. Even with morphine, the pain had to be almost unbearable.

When he was finished, Jones said to the on-lookers, "Okay, help me get him to his bunk."

After Jones had made Weir comfortable, he went forward to the wardroom, where Mills and Hunt were pouring over charts of Tokyo Bay. He knocked, walked in, and said, "Weir's in his bunk resting, captain, but I'm afraid he's out for the rest of the patrol. I could only make a try at setting the bone. He can't move it."

Mills exploded. "Of all the damned stupid things to happen, this is the stupidest!"

"You know what I think, captain? The guy's a psycho. I think the wound was self-inflicted. At least subconsciously self-inflicted."

"I didn't know you were a student of Dr. Freud," Hunt put in.

"Doctor who?" Jones said.

"Never mind," Hunt said. "You sound like a psychiatrist."

"Well, anyway," said Mills, "we better hope that radar doesn't go on the fritz."

"Yes," said Hunt. "That's for damn sure."

# CHAPTER FIFTY-ONE

In the after torpedo room, Tony Walker held a group of six men absolutely spellbound with his account of the shore party's narrow escape. He was a natural storyteller, but his tale needed no embellishment.

He concluded in his Alabama drawl, "But what stands out most in my mind is the way the exec handled everything. Cool as a cucumber. That earthquake scared the shit out of me, but he says,

'Don't worry, men. It's just a mild earthquake.' "

It was now 0350, time to change the watch. Some men drifted off, others yawned and turned in to get an hour or two of sleep. Tony Walker gave Lockwood-san her four o'clock feeding, changed her diapers, and rocked the bassinet gently until she drifted off to sleep.

Afterward, he opened the small tin box Red Weaver had given him. It contained the donations to the Lockwood-san Fund. Tony counted the money carefully. It came to $130.50. Counting the $60.00 he had made on the sales of the fishnet sections, the fund now contained $190.50. He closed the box, leaned over the bassinet, and said, "Well, old gal, if we get out of this briar patch alive, you'll have a nice little nest egg to build on."

Wally Yates, the OOD, spoke softly into the bridge intercom: "Report to the captain. Battery charge complete. Sunrise in an hour and a half. It has stopped raining."

"Aye," the speaker responded, repeating the instructions.

Five minutes later, Mills appeared on the bridge. He was groggy, still half asleep. "All quiet?" he asked Yates.

"All quiet, captain."

Mills swept the base and the moored I-boats with his binoculars. Then he said, "Let's pull the cork."

# CHAPTER FIFTY-TWO

They leveled off at periscope depth and trimmed the boat. At the periscope, Mills said, "Morning twilight coming on. Go to battle stations." The order had been anticipated, and most of the men were already at battle stations. In less than one minute, the boat was manned and ready.

"Down scope," Mills said, turning to Hunt. "No sign of unusual activity. It looks like they've let down their guard. We'll go out the same way we came in—beneath a big ship."

"In daylight, captain?" Hunt asked.

"Yes," said Mills. "At the first opportunity. If we screw around here all day, we'll use up the battery. Beyond the net, we've got eight miles in Uraga Suido before we reach open water. We might have to do that leg submerged, and if so, we'd need the battery."

"Aye, aye," said Hunt, concealing his strong reservations. The plan was typical Mauler Mills: damn the torpedoes, full speed ahead.

"Give me a course to the net gate," said Mills.

Hunt quickly laid out the course on the chart. "Zero-nine-five."

"Make it so," Mills said. "All ahead full."

"Slow-speed screws and pinging at zero-four-zero," Jones reported. "Faint."

"Put me on zero-four-zero," Mills said, and Childress swung the periscope to the bearing.

"Visibility still poor," said Mills. "See something! Top-hamper. Mark!"

"Zero-four-two," Childress said.

"Down scope," said Mills.

Childress lowered the scope into the well.

"Too far away," Mills said, walking to the chart table and studying the chart over Hunt's shoulder. Three miles to the net. Average depth: 180 feet. He took off his baseball cap and scratched his head.

Childress watched him anxiously.

"Screws at two-seven-zero," Jones reported.

"Up scope," Mills said. "Two-seven-zero."

He clamped his eye into the rubber mold and adjusted the focus. "I see him," he said. "A destroyer, coming out of the finger piers."

"He's speeding up," said Jones.

"Angle on the bow zero," said Mills. "He's got a bone in his teeth. Down scope."

"High-speed screws at zero-zero-zero," Jones reported. "Another destroyer, I think."

"Shit!" Mills said. "Take her deep—150 feet. Rig for silent running."

The third destroyer, outbound from the finger piers, passed directly overhead at high speed. She was not pinging. She drew off to the east—toward the net.

Mills turned to Hunt and said grimly, "The buzzards are gathering." They had obviously not let down their guard.

Shark closed the net at slow speed. From sonar bearings and careful periscope observations, they saw that the three destroyers had formed a picket line just inside the net gate. They were cruising back and forth slowly, pinging. It would be suicidal to attempt to slip out the gate beneath a ship. The destroyers would pounce instantly, nailing them on the spot or bottling them up in Uraga Suido.

After another quick periscope observation, Mills said, "The door is definitely closed. Back to the drawing board."

Mills studied the chart again. Suddenly he stabbed a forefinger on the penciled-in net at a place just north of the old fort on Daisan Kaiho, the southern anchor of the net. "We've got a hundred feet of water here," he said. "Let's cut our way out."

Hunt studied the chart. It was a mere half mile from the net gate—and the destroyer pickets—to Daisan Kaiho. One thousand yards. The odds of being detected were high, but Hunt had no alternative to suggest.

They had brought wire-cutting gear against this contingency. It had been entrusted to *Shark's* unofficial diver, Tony Walker.

"We'll need a volunteer to help Walker," said Mills. "A strong swimmer."

Later, reliving that moment, Childress could never understand why he did it. He concluded it was most likely out of sheer terror, the lunge of a trapped rat.

"Captain, I'm a strong swimmer," he said.

Mills appraised Childress with a probing glance. "You are, huh?"

"Yes, sir," said Childress. "Very strong. I've done a lot of goggle diving."

"Are you volunteering?" Mills asked. "You understand the risks?"

"Yes, sir."

"Very well," said Mills. "Lay below and see Walker. Tell him to prepare the diving and cutting gear."

"Aye, aye, sir."

# CHAPTER FIFTY-THREE

Closing the southern leg of the net at creeping speed, *Shark* turned southeast, twenty feet off the bottom.

"Rig for silent running," said Mills. "All hands absolutely quiet."

The telephone talker passed the word, almost in a whisper. It was so quiet they could hear the water gently swishing through the periscope shears.

At the sonar stack, Doc Jones kept watch on the bearings of the three patrolling destroyers who were pinging steadily. The screws and pinging could be heard through *Shark*'s hull.

"Up scope," Mills said, turning the focus to high and examining the water ahead. It was murky, the visibility poor. "How far is it?" he asked.

"Estimated five hundred yards," said Hunt.

"Are Walker and Childress ready?"

"In the escape trunk, captain," Hunt replied. "Diving gear rigged, cutting gear ready."

"All right," said Mills. "Sixty-five feet."

The shallow-water diving rig—a face mask and air hose tethered to the boat—would not operate at one hundred feet, and the cutting would have to be done as shallow as possible, just below periscope depth.

"Watch your depth!" Mills said quietly, eye on the depth-gauge needle. "Don't broach."

"Aye, aye," control stage-whispered. Then, "Sixty-five feet."

Jones momentarily stopped turning the sonar

head, settling on a bearing directly astern. "What the hell is *that?*" he said aloud.

"What?" said Mills.

"A strange noise aft," Jones said excitedly. "Sounds like it's shipboard. Captain! It's Lockwood-san, bawling!"

"Shut that baby up," Mills said quietly but firmly.

In the after torpedo room, Seaman Neal, who had again assumed responsibility for Lockwood-san, was frantic. He had the baby in his arms, rocking her back and forth, but she refused to be calmed.

The telephone talker said, "Captain says to shut her up. They can hear her on sonar."

"She's hungry," Neal said desperately. "I can't find her bottle."

"It's probably in the refrigerator," a torpedoman said.

"Captain says to shut her up *immediately!*" the telephone talker said. "Put a fist in her mouth, if necessary."

"Take her to the galley," said the torpedoman.

Neal ran forward to the galley with the screaming baby, passing through the maneuvering room, the two engine rooms, the empty crew's sleeping compartment.

"Get her bottle!" the wild-eyed Neal shouted at Freddie Lyman.

Lyman found the bottle in the refrigerator. "You should heat it first," he said.

But Neal paid no heed as he forced the cold nipple into the baby's mouth. She chewed the nipple, gave a deep sigh, and began sucking contentedly.

Mills stared anxiously at Jones and the sonar stack.

Jones said, "All quiet aft, sir. But number two destroyer has speeded up and shifted to short-scale pinging. He *heard* us, captain. He's got us. Steady bearing!"

"Left full rudder," said Mills. "All ahead full. Take her deep. Rig for depth charges. Get Walker and Childress out of the escape trunk."

They leveled off at 90 feet, pulling away from the net at full speed, but they could not elude the destroyer. She had them dead to rights.

The first salvo was almost directly on target. WHAM! WHAM! WHAM! WHAM! WHAM! WHAM! *Shark* reeled violently, her metal twisting and groaning. Glass dials in the conning tower shattered.

"Right full rudder," said Mills. "All stop."

"After torpedo room flooding," the telephone talker reported matter-of-factly.

"How bad?"

"The pressure hull is dimpled," the talker replied. "The leak is not yet determined."

"Damage-control party to the after torpedo room," Mills said.

The second salvo was even closer than the first, and they heard one charge clang off the deck before it exploded. Six more explosions shook the boat.

All hands in the conning tower were thrown off their feet; the steel deck plates seemed to rise a foot; seawater gushed down the periscope packing gland. Later, Frank Nalle insisted that the bridge hatch was lifted off its seating an inch or so, but no water came down.

"Holy smoke!" Mills gasped. "That guy must be the dean of the Tokyo Sonar School."

"Damage control reports after room flooding heavily," the telephone talker reported. "All other compartments secure. No serious damage."

"Rig in the sound heads," said Mills. "Put her on the bottom."

*Shark* settled soundlessly into the murky bottom, 120 feet down. They shut down all machinery and propulsion. But the destroyer was not fooled. She delivered a third salvo, directly on target. WHAM! WHAM! WHAM! WHAM!

WHAM! WHAM! Again *Shark* reeled violently, then pitched bow-first into the mud, pounding and shuddering.

"Release fuel oil," Mills said, "and heavy air bubbles. Put some mattresses and debris out the torpedo tubes. Make it look good."

It was an old trick they had rehearsed in drills many times, and the captain's orders were carried out promptly and efficiently. Looking through the periscope, Mills could see the oil, bubbles, and debris rising to the surface.

"Screws stopped," Jones reported. "She's lying to, almost overhead."

The Japanese would be probing the debris and oil, and with any luck at all, the ruse would work. As Hunt had said, the Japanese were notoriously careless and not terribly persistent when it came to antisubmarine warfare. Much too eager to claim a killing and call it a day.

"She's starting up," Jones reported, and they all held their breath. "Pulling off."

"Damage control reports severe flooding in the after torpedo room, captain," the telephone talker said. "Ankle-deep."

"Put high-pressure air in the after room," said Mills. "Abandon the compartment."

"She's definitely pulling away," Jones said. "Not even pinging."

"They can't abandon the compartment, sir," the talker said. "The watertight door is jammed."

Mills stared stonily at the telephone talker as though it were all his fault.

"Water is waist-deep, sir," the talker said. "Air pressure seems to be holding the water at that level."

"He's gone," Jones said. "Back to the picket line."

"Okay," said Mills, turning to the talker. "Is there any further word on the watertight door?"

"Hopelessly jammed, sir," the talker said. "Twelve men in the compartment."

"Very light screws approaching," said Jones. "Small craft. Liberty boat or harbor patrol."

"To pick up the debris," said Mills. "And to verify the kill."

His mind was riveted on the crisis in the flooding after torpedo room. Twelve men trapped, water to their waists. Tons and tons of water. Somehow the men had to be gotten out; the weight of tons of water had to be compensated for.

"Screws overhead," said Jones. "Stopped."

The after torpedo room deck hatch could be converted to an escape hatch by lowering a brass sleeve almost to the deck and then adjusting the inside pressure to seawater pressure. Thus equalized, a man with a Momsen lung could duck underwater, go up the sleeve, open the hatch, and float to the surface—right into the hands of the Japanese in the liberty launch.

Hunt spoke up. "Captain, what if we rigged a line from the after torpedo room hatch to the forward escape trunk? The men could get out with Momsen lungs, pull themselves along the line, then enter the forward torpedo room through the escape trunk."

Mills considered this proposal for a full minute. Such an operation was so perilous he almost dismissed the idea summarily. All hands had simulated that kind of escape with Momsen lungs in the sub school's hundred-foot-deep tank tower. But it was one thing to do something like that in warm water under the watchful supervision of instructors, quite another to do it in the murky, icy waters of Tokyo Bay. But what else could they do? At length he said, "All right. Let's give it a try. We need two strong swimmers."

"Walker and Childress," said Hunt.

"See if they'll volunteer."

# CHAPTER FIFTY-FOUR

In the escape trunk in the forward torpedo room, Childress adjusted the strap on his Momsen lung face mask. The flow of oxygen was clean and cool. By now, the flooding water had reached his waist. He looked at Tony Walker, whose face was likewise obscured by a mask, and Walker flashed him an "okay" sign with his hand. Childress returned the sign, although far from feeling okay; he was nearly paralyzed with anxiety.

The icy water flooded over their heads and they both popped their ears by swallowing hard. When the pressure inside the lock equalized with the outside pressure, Walker undogged the escape trunk door, and they swam out, each holding a powerful underwater lantern. When they reached the upper deck, Childress swam aft with the looped bitter end of the line and Walker remained by the escape trunk to anchor his end of the line.

Childress swam purposefully and rapidly in the inky water, breathing hard into his mask. In spite of the heavy clothing he wore, his body was numb from the cold, but he was calmer now. Water was his natural element. The light played along the wood-slat deck; then he saw the bridge and the afterdeck gun; and in less than thirty seconds he reached the closed after torpedo room hatch.

He quickly tied the rope to a steel eye that

protruded from the deck, paused a moment, and tested the line. It was taut. Walker had anchored the other end. He took another deep breath and pulled himself hand over hand toward the bridge. When he looked up he saw that the water was polluted with oil. Faintly he could hear a small engine. The liberty launch, pulling off. He passed the bridge and pulled himself along the forward deck where Walker was hanging on the line, waiting. Childress flashed him an "okay" sign, and Walker returned it.

They swam back into the escape trunk, dogged the door, and while Walker opened the lower drain, Childress bled air into the chamber, forcing the water down the drain. In a moment or two, the chamber was dry. Childress secured the air, Walker opened the lower hatch, and they climbed down the ladder into the forward torpedo room, shivering uncontrollably.

"Line secure," Walker reported through chattering teeth to Hunt, who had taken station in the forward torpedo room.

"Good work," Hunt said. He turned to the telephone talker. "Report line in place to the captain."

Mills did not have to be told. He had watched Walker and Childress through the periscope, silently urging them on. He replied through the talker, "A hearty well-done to Walker and Childress."

Doc Jones draped cream-colored navy blankets around them and gave them mugs of coffee laced with brandy. "Drink this, take a hot shower, and put on warm clothes," he said.

Mills said to the telephone talker, "Tell the after room to eject all torpedoes. Then abandon the compartment."

There were ten torpedoes in the compartment, four in the tubes, six reloads in the storage skids. The ten weighed about thirteen tons, and jettisoning them would help compensate for the added weight of the seawater.

The twelve men who were sloshing around in the icy waist-deep water in the after torpedo room had already disarmed all ten torpedoes. They ejected the four in the tubes, quickly reloaded another four, ejected these, and finally got rid of the last two. Then they lowered the escape sleeve and built up pressure in the compartment with high-pressure air until the atmosphere matched that of the outside seawater. They put on Momsen lungs and divided themselves into two groups of six, the maximum capacity of the forward escape trunk. Torpedoman Striker Nutting was first up the sleeve, and he undogged the deck hatch.

In the conning tower, Mills fixed the periscope on the after hatch. He saw it open and he saw Nutting come out. Nutting grabbed the line and began pulling himself forward, hand over hand. The other five men came after him, one by one. "Fantastic!" Mills said aloud. "Absolutely fantastic!"

He swung the periscope forward and watched Nutting let go of the line, swim down, and undog the escape trunk door. The other five men came after him, one by one. The door closed.

Several minutes later, the telephone talker said to Mills, "Mr. Hunt reports six men recovered, sir."

"Very well," said Mills. "Tell the second group to commence abandoning the compartment."

He swung the periscope toward the after hatch and saw the next six men coming up, one by one, just like the first group. The last man closed and tightly dogged the hatch, then he worked his way forward along the line.

Five minutes later, the talker said, to Mills, "Mr. Hunt reports the second group recovered. All twelve men from the after room now in the forward room."

"Very well," said Mills. "My compliments to Mr. Hunt—and to the twelve men."

Soon after that, Hunt appeared in the conning tower. "Doc's got them all in hand, captain. Coffee. Brandy. Blankets. Hot showers. They'll sack out in the forward room."

"What a goddamned crew!" said Mills. "All right, let's compensate."

"Blow safety?" said Hunt.

"Yes, blow safety."

Safety was a big emergency ballast tank that was always kept full of water. Emptying safety would compensate for the added weight of the water in the flooded compartment, and they could control the blowing so that no bubbles rose to the surface.

"Blow safety," Hunt shouted to control.

"Blow safety," control reported.

They could hear the hiss of high-pressure air.

"Safety blown to the mark," control reported. "Getting light aft."

"Very well," said Mills. "Bring her off the bottom. Trim the boat."

They came up to a hundred feet. *Shark* was still overly heavy aft, so they pumped dry the after trim tank. The boat was still down by the stern, hanging with a ten-degree up angle. Mills frowned. What to do now?

"Suggest you send all off-watch personnel to the forward torpedo room, captain," said Hunt, adding figures on the pad.

"Good idea," said Mills, passing the word to control.

Thirty-five men joined those already in the forward torpedo room—the normal two-man watch, plus the twelve from the after torpedo room who were bedded down in the bunks. In all, fifty men—equaling four tons in weight. That did the trick. *Shark* leveled off.

Control reported, "Zero bubble," and Mills exhaled a long sigh of relief.

At Mills's request, Doc Jones came to the conning tower to reman the sonar stack. No sooner had he clamped on the earphones than he said, "Captain, slow screws, bearing two-seven-oh."

## CHAPTER FIFTY-FIVE

"Up periscope," said Mills. They were at sixty-five feet. "Put me on two-seven-oh."

Childress, wearing warm, dry clothing and still burning inside from the brandy, put the scope on the bearing. Mills knelt on the deck, exposing only two or three inches of glass. "It's an I-boat coming out of the base," he said. "Angle on the bow zero. Stand by. Mark! Down scope. Take her down to one hundred feet."

They maneuvered *Shark* slowly and carefully. With the after room flooded, she was clumsy and a bit skittish, apt to take bigger angles than they desired.

"I-boat's submerging," Jones reported.

Mills listened in the spare earphone. He could hear the rush of air through her vents, the clank of the main induction closing.

"One hundred feet," control reported. "Holding steady, sir."

"Very well," said Mills. "Right full rudder, ahead two-thirds."

They lay on the track of the oncoming I-boat. Best to move to one side, Mills thought. But why had the I-boat submerged?

"She's pinging, captain," Jones reported.

Childress felt a stab of terror. No, no, no, he said to himself, biting his lower lip. Not this.

"Rudder amidships," said Mills. "All ahead full."

"Still pinging," said Jones.

"Single ping on her," said Mills. "Try to overlap her ping."

Jones carried out these orders with precision, and *Shark's* ping intermingled with the ping of the I-boat. It probably would not be noticed.

"Five-oh-oh-oh yards," said Jones. Two and a half miles.

"What the hell is going on, Bill?" said Mills, turning to Hunt. "Why should she submerge? Why should she be pinging?"

Hunt thought a moment. "The destroyer claims a kill. It's the second claim for a kill in as many days, with very little proof. You know the tin can operators. Say you are in charge of security for the human torpedoes. You simply don't believe the claims. So you send one of your I-boats to search the area thoroughly, to confirm by sonar that there really has been a kill. Put yourself in their shoes. Wouldn't you do the same?"

Mills pondered this scenerio, then he frowned. "Yes, I would. I'd send out my best skipper, the first team."

"Still pinging," Jones reminded.

"Very well," said Mills. "Left full rudder." They would head toward the base, presenting the smallest possible silhouette to the oncoming I-boat.

"Bearing steady," said Jones.

"All stop," said Mills. "Rig for silent running." He added, "And not a peep out of that baby."

They drifted along slowly, coming to a stop, but it was difficult to hold *Shark's* depth with no way on.

"We're bow heavy now, captain," control reported. "Request we put some way on."

"Send five men aft," Mills said.

When that was done, control reported, "Zero bubble, captain. Holding."

"Still pinging," Jones said. "He's got us! Short-scale!"

"Christ!" said Mills. "Go to battle stations—no—Belay that. We've got to keep those men forward."

"Stopped pinging," Jones reported. "Screws stopped."

"Mmmmmmmmm," Mills said, scratching his head. He had never faced a duel with a submerged submarine. No skipper had. Not the real thing. It was like two blindfolded men in a blacked-out room going at each other with loaded pistols.

"Make ready tubes one, two, and three. Open the outer doors." He turned to Bell and Yates on TDC. They had been plotting the bearings—and the single range—into the machine, but they had not received enough data.

"Captain!" Jones said. "I heard a loud clanking at one-eight-zero."

"That's her," Mills said. "What depth?" Other than Jones's intuition, there was no way to determine depth.

"I'd guess sixty feet," Jones said. "Periscope depth."

"Come up to sixty feet," Mills said.

They came up slowly, dumping water overboard from the trim system.

"More clanking," Jones reported. "One-eight-zero."

"What the hell could it be?" Mills demanded.

"Don't have any idea," Jones said. "Never heard anything like it on a submarine."

"Sixty feet," control reported. "Holding. Zero bubble."

"Very well," said Mills. "Up scope."

He made a quick 360-degree sweep, but he could see nothing unusual. "Down scope."

"Captain," said Hunt, "I think I know what that clanking might be."

"Well? What is it?"

"She could be releasing a human-guided torpedo from its cradle," Hunt said. "They used heavy rigging to strap them in the cradles. We couldn't tell what it was, but it would be noisy to unshackle, I'm sure."

Absolute silence fell over the conning tower.

"Give me a single ping," Mills said. That would give their position away to an alert sonar operator, but it was imperative to know the range and bearing.

The ping was loud, clear, metallic. Jones reported, "Bearing one-eight-zero. Range two-oh-oh-oh." One mile.

"Left full rudder, ahead one-third," Mills said. "Steady on one-eight-zero. Zero angle on the bow."

Bell and Yates cranked the pitifully limited data into the TDC. Never had Bell felt so uncertain about the setup TDC was generating. "Zero gyro," he said. "Generated range one-five-oh-oh."

"All stop!" Mills said.

"Screws," Jones reported. "One-eight-zero."

"What kind of screws?" Mills said.

"High-speed," Jones said. "A torpedo. Belay that. Like a torpedo, but slower."

"It wouldn't be as fast," Hunt said. "I'm afraid this is it, captain."

"Stand by one, two, and three," Mills said.

"Standing by," the telephone talker said. "Outer doors open."

Childress felt faint. His premonition had been correct. He would not live out the day—not even the next minute. Then, suddenly, a vast calm fell over him. Peace. It was over now. There was nothing more he could do about it.

"Continuous pinging," Mills said to Jones.

The signals, one behind the other, probed the water. "Contact at one-eight-zero. Double return, captain. The I-boat's dead on us. Nose to nose. The torpedo is between us. Range one-two-oh-oh." A little over half a mile.

"Very well," Mills said with amazing calm. "We'll let the range close to—no! *Fire one! Fire two! Fire three!*" He had nearly miscalculated. Even now it might be too late.

The three torpedoes swished out of the tubes, leaving *Shark* momentarily light up front, and her bow rose sharply.

"Get the bow down!" Mills yelled. "Get those five men forward again."

Childress was oblivious of everything except the ticking stopwatch. His whole being centered on the jerking sweep hand. But he could not calculate the run. One torpedo closing another, perhaps at a combined speed of eighty knots . . .

*BOOM!*

It came before Jones could get his earphones off, and he doubled up in pain, holding his head. The shock wave was immense, terrifying, paralyzing. *Shark* was literally pushed downward as though by a giant hand. She hit bottom with a terrible crash, and everyone was thrown to the deck.

"Jesus H. Christ!" Mills cried. "All compartments report."

The damage reports came through the telephone talker immediately: there was countless minor damage, but nothing major.

"Leave her on the bottom," Mills said. "Get the men out of the forward room."

Shaking his head in bewilderment, Childress sat on the chart-table stool. He was still alive, after all.

"Christ!" said Mills, shaking his head ruefully. "They must have huge warheads. Never felt anything like that."

The sonar stack was useless. The underkeel sound heads were buried in the mud, or more likely, wiped off. Still, they could hear the I-boat screws plainly through the hull. She passed directly overhead, pinging, but she did not stop, and presently she hauled off in the direction of the base.

"She's gone," said Mills, still looking at the overhead. "She thinks she got us."

Hunt sat staring at the deck. He was thinking about the eager young men he had seen on the docks, the I-boat skipper and his exec, the portly senior naval officer. One of those young men was dead now, blown to bits. The others would no doubt be celebrating their victory with sake and delicate ceremonial food. Madness!

"Doc," he heard Mills say exuberantly, "issue a ration of medicinal brandy for all hands."

# CHAPTER FIFTY-SIX

*Shark* lay on the bottom, half buried in mud, for the rest of the day. She was like a tomb. All hands not on watch, including Mills and Hunt, fell into deep, exhausted sleep. The watch standers had little to do other than make meaningless entries in the logbook and pass the time in idle chatter, trying not to think about what lay ahead.

At 1730, the watch messenger woke Mills and Hunt. They met in the wardroom, groggy and sleepy-eyed, and Martinez served them a hot dinner and the captain's favorite desert: ice cream with chocolate sauce and nuts. The meal revived them, and once again they were ready to face the barrier lying between them and the open sea.

"Their guard will be down now for sure," said Mills, lighting his big cigar.

Hunt was not so sure, but he said nothing.

"We'll go back to the line of scrimmage," Mills

went on. "We'll ease up to the gate and slip out beneath a ship."

"You want a full battery charge, captain?" Hunt asked.

"No. Forget that. We'll get in what charge we can. What I want is to get the hell out of here! We'll slip through the gate, go down Uraga Suido on the surface, or maybe at radar depth."

Hunt would have preferred the battery charge, to be on the safe side, but again he expressed no reservations.

"Let's go!" said Mills, getting up and crushing his cigar in a brass ashtray.

They went to the conning tower where Wally Yates and others of the watch were sitting around quietly swapping sea stories.

"I'll take the conn, Wally," Mills said affably.

"Aye, captain," said Yates. "Nothing to report, sir. Stuck on the bottom in 120 feet."

"All ahead full," Mills ordered. "Periscope depth."

*Shark*'s two screws pounded heavily in the mud, shaking the boat, and she broke loose and nosed up.

"Heavy aft," control reported.

"Get some men forward," Mills said.

"Captain, I can't hear a thing," said the sonar operator. "The gear's out of commission."

"We wiped off the sound heads all right," Mills said, frowning. "Secure the sonar."

The telephone barked. Hunt answered. It was the maneuvering room. He listened, hung up, and said to Mills, "Maneuvering reports the port shaft knocked out of line. Squealing badly."

"I'm not surprised," Mills said with a calm that amazed everyone. "The charge that got the after room also got that shaft." There was nothing to be done about it.

"Periscope depth," control said.

"Up scope," said Mills.

He made a quick sweep of the horizon. He saw the running lights of the two net tenders close by and the distant lights of the base.

"Radar depth," Mills ordered.

They planed up to thirty-five feet.

"Radar depth," control reported.

"Man the SJ," Mills said.

The radar operator turned on the set, waited for the tube to warm, then began the sweep. "Sir, there's something wrong with the display scope," he said.

Mills left the periscope and stared down at the SJ display scope. It was a blizzard of white snow.

"Secure the radar," he said grimly. "Surface!"

They came up slowly, and Mills cracked and opened the hatch and ran to the bridge, inhaling the fresh air. He swept his binoculars slowly around the horizon. The lookouts, the quartermaster, and Hunt were behind him.

"All clear port."

"Running lights on the net tenders starboard."

"All clear aft."

"Very well," Mills said to the lookouts. Then to the intercom; "Propulsion on one main engine. Charge batteries on three. Ahead one-third."

He turned to Hunt, "Course to the gate?"

"Zero-four-zero."

"Come left to zero-four-zero."

A lookout shouted, "Ship, bearing three-three-oh relative!"

"What kind of ship?" Mills shouted.

"A destroyer, sir!" the lookout cried. "Coming dead on. Two, three miles."

"Clear the bridge!" Mills shouted. "Dive! Dive!"

They leveled off at a hundred feet, heavy in the stern. The destroyer apparently had not seen them, and it crossed over them at high speed. They could hear the screws through the hull. It was going too fast to ping, and it pulled off to the southwest.

"What do you think?" Mills asked Hunt.

"I think the picket's still in place, captain," Hunt said. "They haven't let down their guard yet."

# CHAPTER FIFTY-SEVEN

Al Weir lay in his bunk, groggy from the morphine, his mind segueing from fantasy to fantasy. He felt a hand on his shoulder, then heard a distant voice.

"Weir?"

It was unmistakably the captain. Weir opened his eyes to find a flashlight beam on his face.

"Sorry to bother you," said Mills. "We've had a radar casualty." He paused to let that sink in. "I don't think we can get out of here without the SJ."

Weir stared at the captain and the flashlight. "What's wrong?" he said thickly.

"The display scope is nothing but snow."

"Oh my," said Weir, his mind now registering. "Oh my."

Mills said, "Nobody has a clue about how to fix it."

Weir propped himself up on his elbow, staring at Mills. "Help me up."

"No, no," said Mills. "If you could just *tell* Gilsey what to do, maybe—"

"Gilsey!" Weir sneered. "That imbecile? I wouldn't let him get within ten feet of my gear. Captain! Help me up. Get me to the conning-tower."

Before Mills could protest again or think of a new tack, Weir was half lifting himself out of the bunk. Mills turned to Hunt, who was standing behind him, and said, "Give us a hand."

While Mills lifted Weir by the armpits, Hunt held his legs out level, or as level as he could, and they edged out of the sleeping area into the passageway, then into the crew's mess. Four hands leaped up to help, but Mills dismissed them. He and Hunt carried Weir on to the control room and stopped beneath the conning-tower hatch. How would they get him up the ladder?

Bob Pierpont provided the solution. He quickly fashioned a chest harness of half-inch line, and they put the harness on Weir, ran the line to the conning tower, and pulled him up slowly. The pain was almost more than Weir could bear. He cried out, his eyes bulged, his tongue came out. They laid him out on a mattress in front of the SJ.

"Get my tool kit," he gasped, and Pierpont went to fetch it.

For a full hour, Weir lay on his side on the mattress, working on the SJ. Pierpont served as his orderly and go-fer, handing him tools, rooting out spare parts. All the while, Weir was in intense pain, grunting and moaning, occasionally crying out. For Mills, it was one of the strangest interludes of the war. He couldn't help feeling sorry for the man, nor could he keep from admiring Weir's guts.

"That's it," Weir announced, lying flat on his back, gasping and moaning.

"Fixed?" Mills said anxiously, concealing his mountain of doubt.

"Sir," Weir said. "That's it."

Mills caught his breath. Weir had never before said sir.

"You're sure?" Mills pressed. He wanted to test the radar before they took him back because there was no way the man could stand another trip to the conning tower.

"When I say something is fixed," Weir said

through gritted teeth, "you can believe it's *fixed,* damn it!"

"Very well," said Mills, ignoring the surliness. "Let's get him back to his bunk."

They lowered Weir to the control room, then carried him back to his bunk. He was in agonizing pain, crying out continuously.

Mills summoned Doc Jones and said, "Give him more morphine." Jones gave Weir another injection, then felt the leg very gently. The sheered fibula had punched through the skin. He dusted the wound with sulfa powder and said to Mills, "Captain, he can't be moved again. There's real danger that the artery could be cut."

# CHAPTER FIFTY-EIGHT

"Radar depth," ordered Mills.

At thirty-five feet, the SJ operator turned on the set. The display scope was normal again. "SJ back in operation," he said.

"What do you see?" asked Mills, standing behind the operator.

The operator read off the contacts. There were five. The two net tenders, and slightly to the west of the net, three more brighter pips in a north-south line. Mills leaned over the scope. The three pips in a line, he knew, were the destroyer pickets.

"Secure the radar," he said. "Periscope depth."

Now what? Hunt wondered. There was no getting through the gate, that was clear. He stared at the chart, studying the penciled-in net and the minefield running south from the old fort on

Daisan Kaiho to the shore. The minefield was a mile and a quarter long, and the water depth averaged 150 feet. Suddenly an idea struck. "Can you come here for a second, captain?" he said urgently.

Mills leaned heavily over the chart table.

"Here's the minefield," said Hunt, tracing it with his finger. "It lies north and south. I have an idea it's not very wide. What would happen if we fired a full salvo of torpedoes into the field?"

Mills stared at the chart, pursing his lips. Then he sat down, and they discussed the pros and cons for a full half hour. When they were done, Mills stepped to the PA mike.

"All hands. This is the captain. The net gate is solidly blocked by three tin cans. With our port shaft squealing like it is and the sonar knocked out, I don't think we'd stand much of a chance getting out that way. We feel the best way out is through the minefield. We're going to blast a passageway with a full salvo of torpedoes, then go through behind them." He paused. "There is more than ordinary risk involved. You should be prepared to abandon ship if necessary. Make all preparations and govern yourselves accordingly." Another pause. "With God's help, we'll get out."

He turned to Hunt. "Burn all the code books and confidential papers."

In the chiefs' quarters, Wheeler smiled wanly and said to Pierpont, "The end of the road, buddy."

"Yes," Pierpont said. "This is it. I guess filthy-mouth Corley had a good point about that female. Ever since she's been on board . . ."

# CHAPTER FIFTY-NINE

At periscope depth, *Shark* crept southeast toward the minefield, navigating by the net tenders and the breakwater lights. A half hour before midnight, Hunt said, "I think this is far enough, captain."

"Very well," Mills said. "Surface."

They came up sluggishly, and Mills led the watch to the bridge. He spoke into the intercom: "Turn on the SJ. Mr. Hunt, check your navigation, please."

Working with the radar data, Hunt plotted a precise fix. He reported to Mills, "Right on the money, captain."

"Very well," Mills said. "My compliments, Mr. Hunt. I'll get us through the field, you take us down Uraga Suido."

"Aye, aye, captain."

They had decided to go through the field on the surface. Should anything go wrong—should they hit an unexploded mine—the men would have a slightly better chance of survival. A few might get off. If they hit a mine submerged, no one would survive.

"Propulsion on all four main engines," Mills said. "Start the low-pressure blowers. Blow all ballast tanks dry. Stand by the forward tubes."

Hunt came to the bridge. "I had one last thought, captain."

"Yes?" Mills said.

"Should we break radio silence and tell the admiral what we found here?"

"You destroyed the code books."

"In the clear, I meant."

"The Japs would pick it up," Mills said. "They'd know we knew. I wouldn't want to tell them that. What's the matter? Don't you have confidence in your scheme?"

"It was just a thought."

"Well, no need for it," Mills said. "I'll bring us out. Maybe not in one piece, but out."

"Captain, I have every confidence that you will."

"And by the way, Mr. Hunt," said Mills, "I have every confidence in you."

"Every, sir?"

"Every," said Mills. "You're the goddamnedest lawyer I ever met."

Hunt went below, glowing with satisfaction.

"All right, men," Mills said on the PA system, "go to battle stations. I want each and every one of you to give his utmost. Let's go."

Into the intercom he said: "Open the outer doors on all forward tubes."

"Outer doors open."

"Two-degree spread," Mills said. "Zero gyro, depth set fifteen feet. Five-second intervals."

"Aye, aye." It had all been carefully rehearsed, every detail worked out.

"Fire!" said Mills.

The torpedoes swished out at five-second intervals. One. Two. Three. Four. Five. Six.

"All tubes fired electrically."

"Very well," said Mills, his binoculars fixed on the six torpedo wakes. "Running hot, straight, and normal. All ahead emergency. Rudder amidships. Keep her on zero-nine-zero. Commence reloading all tubes forward."

"Thirty seconds," Childress reported on the intercom.

*Shark* slowly picked up speed. Mills could feel the breeze on his face, first faintly, then gradually building in force. Go. Go. Go.

"Captain, that number three picket is increasing speed," radar reported. "Coming our way." He gave the range and bearing.

"Okay," Mills said. "Keep an eye on him."

"Sixty seconds," Childress reported.

"Hit, goddamn it!" Mills demanded into the wind. *"Hit!"*

As if in obedience to his command, the dark sea ahead erupted in flame and fire. An awesome geyser of water rose two hundred feet into the sky.

"A hit!" Mills cried triumphantly.

"We heard it," Hunt said. "And felt it."

A second violent explosion erupted dead ahead.

"Another hit!" Mills shouted.

"Ballast blown dry," control reported. It was Pierpont.

"Secure the low-pressure blower," Mills replied.

"Making 20.9 knots," the helmsman Frank Nalle said. "Steady on zero-nine-zero."

A third explosion tore the sea apart on the starboard bow. "Another hit!" Mills shouted.

"We should be well within the field by now," said Hunt.

"Incoming mail!" cried one of the lookouts.

The shell wooshed by, struck the water two hundred yards off the port bow, and blew up with indescribable force. Mills yelled maniacally into the intercom: "The destroyer's gunning, *Shark's* running. Goddamn! They hit a mine!"

Three more shells woosh over the bridge and fell ahead, kicking up geysers of water. Mills held to a steady, straight course, following the wake of the torpedoes. There could be no "chasing splashes" in a minefield.

"Clear the bridge!" Mills shouted to the lookouts, and they raced below.

"Halfway through the field," Hunt reported.

"Twenty-one knots," Nalle said.

Mills couldn't believe it. The engines must be dancing off the mounts.

A shell from the destroyer struck another mine a hundred yards dead ahead. The explosion shook Shark from bow to stern, and a Niagara of water smashed the bridge, knocking Mills to the deck.

"All right, captain." Hunt asked anxiously on the intercom.

"Okay," Mills gasped, getting to his feet. "It was so close I could read Red Weaver's name on it."

"Destroyer's stopped," radar reported.

"He wouldn't be fool enough to follow us in here," Mills responded.

Three more shells wooshed over Shark. All fell close off the port bow, kicking up geysers. One struck another mine which blew up with immense force, skewing Shark's bow thirty degrees to starboard.

"Mind your helm!" Mills cried.

Nalle threw the helm hard to port, and Shark swung smartly back on course. Mills stared transfixed at the waters to starboard. A horned mine passed down the side, not more than ten feet off the saddle tanks.

"We should be beyond the field," Hunt reported.

"That's what you think," Mills said. "It's wider than we figured."

Two more shells fell close, a beautiful straddle, port and starboard, fifty yards astern. A slight range adjustment, Mills thought, and . . .

"Dive! Dive!" he cried, racing for the hatch.

Shark went under like an express train, so quickly that Mills was drenched closing the hatch.

"Twenty degrees down bubble," he said. "One hundred feet."

The bow tilted sharply and steeply down, dangerously so.

"Watch your bubble!" Hunt shouted.

"They had us dead on," Mills said to Hunt. Mills was short of breath. "Too damned close."

"One hundred feet," control reported. *Shark* leveled out, hanging heavy by the stern.

"All ahead one-third," said Mills. "Continue on zero-nine-zero." Then to Hunt, "The whole god-damned Jap navy is going to be waiting for us in Uraga Suido."

The eerie quiet was shattered by an unworldly scraping noise outside on the hull, forward on the port side.

"All stop!" Mills shouted. "All back emergency. That's a mine cable!"

All hands in the conning tower, except Mills, froze in terror.

"All stop," Mills said, his eyes clear, his mind alert, his voice steady. Watching him, Hunt thought, the man is unhuman. The greater the peril, the cooler he becomes.

They stood transfixed as *Shark* backed and stopped. The steel cable scraped down her side to midships. Then it stopped.

"The trick is to keep it from snagging on us," Mills said calmly. "If it snags and we move, we'll pull the mine right down on top of us." After a moment, he said, "Dead slow ahead."

*Shark* crept forward, barely moving, her heavy stern dragging ungraciously. The mine cable scraped and slithered down the port saddle tanks. Childress could picture the cable snagged, the mine being pulled steadily down, down, down. Then a cataclysmic explosion.

Mills fixed Childress with a grin. "Why are you sweating, Childress? Haven't you had a happy life?"

"Too short, sir," Childress croaked. "Much too short."

Suddenly the awful scraping stopped.

"All ahead full," Mills said. "Periscope depth."

# CHAPTER SIXTY

"Mark!" said Mills.

"One-seven-zero," said Hunt, reading the periscope azimuth.

"That was Kannon Saki Light," Mills said. "Down scope."

Hunt plotted the bearing on the chart of Uraga Suido. "Recommend one-four-zero."

"Make it so," said Mills. "All ahead full."

*Shark* nosed ahead, the pitlog indicating five knots. The water was deeper here, averaging almost 250 feet. The tide in the channel was outbound, giving them an extra two and a half knots, or a true speed over the bottom of seven and a half knots. They would be able to clear the channel and reach open water in a little over an hour.

"Ask Martinez to bring me some coffee," Mills said to the telephone talker, and Martinez appeared almost instantly with a steaming mug.

"Recommend one-eight-zero," said Hunt.

"Make it so," Mills said as he set his mug on the chart table. "Up scope."

Childress raised the scope.

"Mark!" Mills said. "Kannon Saki Light."

"Two-seven-zero," Hunt said.

"Down scope."

*Shark* headed due south down the channel, leaving Kannon Saki Light on the starboard beam. Fifty-five minutes to go, Childress thought. Fifty-five short minutes.

Gilsey stuck his head into the conning tower.

"Captain, the battery's had it. I can't give you any more turns. You'll have to surface."

Mills glared down at Gilsey for a beat, then said, "Goddamn it, Gilsey! Don't you ever have any good news?"

"Sir," Gilsey said defensively, "you never give me a chance to put in a charge."

The lights dimmed as if to underscore Gilsey's pronouncement. They were draining battery power at a fearful rate.

"All stop," Mills ordered.

The pitlog fell off to four knots. Three. Two. One. Zero. It was eerily quiet.

"We could ride the tide out, captain," Hunt suggested.

"That would take two—three hours," said Mills. "I want to get the hell out of here."

"Captain," Jones said, "I hear faint screws." He was sitting on the stool in front of the inoperative sonar gear. He wasn't wearing earphones.

Mills turned to Jones, and Jones held up a hand for silence. Then he said, "Dead ahead."

Childress stared at Jones in wonderment. He could hear nothing.

"Up scope," Mills said.

Childress raised the scope. Mills walked it around, then steadied on dead ahead. He could see nothing.

"They're pinging," Jones said.

The telephone talker said, "Forward torpedo room reports faint pinging dead ahead."

"Very well," said Mills. "Fifty-five feet." This would expose ten feet of periscope, giving Mills much greater range.

"Mark!" he said. "Angle on the bow one-eight-zero. Fleet destroyer. No, belay that. Two destroyers. Patrolling east-west across the channel."

He left the scope raised, walked to the desk, looked at the chart, and said, "Running right across the mouth between Tsurugi Sake and Myogane Sake."

He returned to the scope and after a moment declared, "Three destroyers, not two. Down scope."

Mills paced the conning tower silently, hands behind his back.

"They're certain to have radar," Hunt reminded.

"Yeah," Mills muttered, deep in thought. Then, "How many fish left forward? Seven?"

"Aye," Hunt replied. "Six in the tubes, one reload."

Mills nodded.

They were all silent, mentally reviewing the same set of facts. Three fleet destroyers on full alert. Six torpedoes in the tubes. No battery for evasion. A flooded after torpedo room.

"How much water here?" Mills asked, going to the chart.

"Seventy fathoms," Hunt said. Four hundred twenty feet.

"Make the depth three hundred feet," said Mills. "Bleed high-pressure air into the after room. I don't want another drop of water back there."

"Aye, aye," Pierpont said from control.

"What's your plan, captain?" said Hunt.

"To drift out submerged and avoid the enemy at all costs," Mills said, grinning. Then to control, "Shut down all machinery except the diving planes. Switch to emergency lamps."

Inwardly, Hunt uncoiled. He was surprised. It was not the typical Mauler Mills operation. He had fully expected Mills to surface and attempt to fight his way out against overwhelming odds.

When the dimming lights went out, Childress switched on the emergency lamps, and they sat in the half darkness. There was no sound except the occasional hum of the diving plane motors, and the soft steady hiss of air into the after torpedo room.

"Be sure Lockwood-san has a bottle," Mills stage-whispered to control.

"Three hundred feet," control reported. "Securing air to the after room. Very heavy aft, sir." There was no sound now, none at all.

"Send men to the forward torpedo room," Mills said quietly.

The minutes dragged by. Presently they could all hear the *thump-thump* and the high-pitched pinging of the slowly patrolling destroyers. Hunt plotted *Shark*'s estimated position yard by yard, using a tidal speed of two and a half knots. It was agonizingly slow.

WHAM! WHAM! WHAM! WHAM! WHAM! WHAM!

The charges fell nearby and above. *Shark* rolled gently. Childress thought his hair literally stood on end.

"They're just speculating," Mills said casually. "They don't have us."

An hour passed. Then two. The screws and pinging drew aft, growing fainter. They could feel the surge of a heavy sea, open water. Mills said, "Periscope depth."

The planesmen put the planes on hard rise, but *Shark* would not plane up. They pumped the trim system dry, but still she would not rise.

"Too little way," said Pierpont. "Permission to blow negative?"

"Blow negative," said Mills. "Carefully, Bob. Start her up and then flood negative." It was a tricky maneuver in any boat, doubly tricky in *Shark*'s stricken state.

"Aye, aye, sir."

They heard a sharp hiss of high-pressure air. "Blowing negative," Pierpont said.

*Shark* began to rise slowly, then astonishingly picking up momentum: 290 feet; 270, 230, 190 . . .

"Flood negative," Mills shouted.

"Aye, aye," said Pierpont. "Secure the blow! Flooding negative."

But *Shark* was out of control, rising to the surface like an express elevator.

"One hundred feet!" Pierpont shouted. "Negative flooded. Can't hold her, captain."

"Full down on the planes," said Mills.

"Eighty feet," Childress called off. "Sixty . . ."

"We're going to broach!" Hunt cried.

"Well, shit!" Mills said with monumental disgust.

It was the first operational foul-up of the patrol. At another time and place it could have been fatal. Here, approaching open water, with the destroyers well astern, it was merely dangerous.

Shark popped to the surface like a giant elongated cork, then settled heavily in the water.

"Surface!" Mills shouted, lunging for the hatch. "Put all main engines on the line. Turn on the SJ. Range to the destroyers."

He opened the hatch and ran to the bridge, sweeping the horizon with his binoculars. The lookouts, and Childress and Hunt came up after him.

"Range to destroyers, one-one-oh-oh-oh," radar reported. Five and a half miles.

"All ahead emergency," Mills said. "Come left to one-nine-zero."

He kept his binoculars fixed on the distant patch of water where the destroyers were patrolling. "Range to the destroyers?"

"Opening out, sir," radar reported. "One-two-five-oh-oh."

"Keep an eye on them," Mills said needlessly.

"Aye, aye, sir."

Childress focused his binoculars on the dark open seas dead ahead. Shark was plunging along at full tilt, the sharp narrow bow rising and falling, occasionally digging in and flinging a stinging spray against the bridge. It was the grandest sight Childress had ever seen, and he silently reveled in the spray.

"Well, Childress," Mills said, "looks like your life may last a little longer after all."

## CHAPTER SIXTY-ONE

They ran south-southeast for a full hour at emergency speed—20.5 knots—crossing the outer Tokyo Bay, Sagami Wan. O Shima lay five miles dead ahead.

"All ahead full," Mills said. Then, "Belay that. Ahead standard on two main engines, charge batteries on two main engines." He turned to Childress. "Ask Mr. Hunt to give me a course to Mikura Jima."

"Aye, aye," said Childress, going below immediately.

"Captain," Hunt said presently, from the control room, "course to Mikura Jima one-eight-zero. Distance six zero miles."

"Steer one-eight-zero."

"Aye, aye."

*Shark* swung left gently to a due south course into the Nampo Shoto, making twelve knots, standard speed on two engines. Her automatic zig-zagger was engaged, and she left a ragged wake.

"Secure from battle stations," Mills said. "Station the regular watch." That was the twelve-to-four. Jim Bell took the deck.

"Bridge," control reported, "we're in the Nojima Sake radar sector now. APR is picking up strong signals at 153 megacycles."

"Very well," said Mills.

"It's a funny signal," control went on. "Not like we had coming in, sir. It's like it's pulsing."

"Pulsing?" Mills said.

"Yes, sir."

"Very well." Then to Bell, "Think I'll go below and get something to eat. Give me a holler when you've got Mikura Jima on radar."

"Aye, aye, sir," said Bell.

"And keep an eye on that Nojima Sake radar," Mills added. "They'll be looking for us."

"Aye."

They steamed steadily south, keeping to the east of the upper Nampo Shoto islands: To Shima, Nii Shima, Kozu Shima. It was a pleasant night, clear and starry, with calm seas. Hunt came to the conning tower every fifteen minutes to make a radar fix and, occasionally, to recommend a slight alteration in course.

At 0331, as Childress later logged it, there was a piercing cry from one of the lookouts: "Aircraft! Coming up astern!"

No sooner were the words out of his mouth than three bright airborne searchlights snapped on. There were three planes in tight formation, barely fifty feet off the water.

"Right full rudder!" Bell cried. "All ahead flank!"

The planes came boring in from astern, pulled up sharply, and roared over the periscope shears. They were so close that the prop wash blew Bell's cap off.

"Clear the bridge! Clear the bridge!" Bell cried out. "Dive! Dive!"

*Shark*, all ballast tanks bone-dry, went down sluggishly, "hanging" as usual at thirty-six feet. They had only reached fifty feet when the three bombs fell. WHAM! WHAM! WHAM!

The hits were close and violent, and Childress was thrown across the conning tower against number one periscope.

"All compartments report damage," Bell said on the PA. "Two hundred feet."

Mills stormed up into the conning tower. "What the hell was that?"

"Aircraft," said Bell. "Flying right on the deck. Radar didn't pick them up."

There was no major damage.

"Two hundred feet!"

"Captain," Bell said, "just as they reached us, they switched on searchlights. They knew exactly where we were."

Mills pondered this news.

"Captain," said Bell after a time, "I think they've developed some way of homing on our SJ radar."

"It looks that way," Mills said, "but how the hell could they do it?"

"I don't know, sir," said Bell. It was indeed an electronic mystery. And if true, a major new menace to the sub force.

They remained at two hundred feet for an hour, then cautiously came up to periscope depth. Mills swept the horizon and then the sky, looking for aircraft exhaust flames. He could see nothing. "All clear," he said. "Surface."

They came up and resumed their southerly course at standard speed, charging batteries on two main engines. Hunt joined them on the bridge, and Mills asked him, "Can you navigate without radar?"

"I think so, captain."

"We're going to secure the radar," Mills said. "Jim has a theory that they're homing on the SJ."

"Let me get a last fix," Hunt said, ducking below.

Using the radar data, he fixed their position. They were five miles north of Miyake Jima. Their outgoing landfall, Mikura Jima, lay twenty miles south of Miyake Jima.

"All right, captain, I've got it," said Hunt.

"Very well," Mills said. "Secure the SJ."

"SJ secured."

"Send Willie Bonsel and Red Weaver to the bridge," said Mills. "I want them on lookout."

Red Weaver had the second best eyes on the boat.

# CHAPTER SIXTY-TWO

They steamed southward. Without radar, Jim Bell felt naked and nervous, even though Bonsel and Weaver were in the shears.

"Fog," Bonsel called from the shears. "Dead ahead."

Bell fixed his binoculars. Looking ahead intently, he could make out the cottony clouds billowing along the dark surface. They had reentered the frigid Kuroshio—the Japan Current.

Bell spoke to the intercom: "Tell the captain we've got fog ahead."

"Aye, aye."

Mills came to the bridge wearing his baseball cap and chewing on a dead cigar.

"Sampan!" Bonsel called out. "Zero-three-zero."

Mills, Bell, and Childress focused their binoculars off the starboard bow. They could see absolutely nothing.

"Willie!" Mills said. "Are you sure?"

"Yes, sir, captain," Bonsel said. "Two-masted. Square stern."

It was a full three minutes before anyone else on the bridge could see the sampan. When Mills at last picked it up, he shouted, "I've got it, Willie! Goddamn! Have you got X-ray vision?"

Bonsel did not reply.

Mills said to Hunt, "We're not far from where we picked up Lockwood-san, are we?"

"No," said Hunt. "As a matter of fact, not more than two, three miles."

"That sampan could be from the same fishing fleet."

"Could be," said Hunt, not getting the captain's drift.

"What would you say to giving Lockwood-san to that sampan?" Mills said. "I hate like hell to take the little critter to Majuro. I mean, what the hell can they do but put her in a POW camp?"

Hunt considered the suggestion. "Yes," he said. "Good idea. And some of the crew will be pleased to get rid of her. Corley, for one."

"All right," Mills said. "Let's do it."

"Carefully," Hunt said.

"Very carefully." Then to the intercom: "Have Walker come to the bridge, please."

Walker appeared within half a minute, and Mills said, "How's Lockwood-san?"

"Very good, sir."

"There's a sampan out there," said Mills. "Probably a sister ship of the one you burned. Would you be terribly disappointed if we returned Lockwood-san to those people?"

Walker was clearly crushed. "I got right close to her, sir."

"Yes, I know," said Mills. "but she'd probably be better off with her own people, don't you think?"

"Yeah," said Walker. "I guess you're right, captain. But what about the fund? I've got 190 bucks already."

"Mmmmmm," said Mills. "We couldn't send it with her. It'd be useless."

"What if Walker converted the money into food from *Shark*'s commissary?" said Hunt. "You could send food with her."

"Yes!" said Mills. "Good idea. Great idea!"

So it was decided. While Walker went below to get Lockwood-san and the food, Mills slowed and maneuvered *Shark* closer to the sampan, and Hunt stood by to translate.

"All stop," said Mills as *Shark* came abreast of the vessel. There was no sign of life.

Hunt put a megaphone to his lips and shouted in Japanese, "Ahoy on the fishing vessel!"

A stooped white-haired man appeared at the rail. He stared at *Shark*, thunderstruck. Then he ran off down the deck, shouting at the top of his lungs.

"We scared the shit out of the sumbitch," Mills said.

A moment later, the old man reappeared. He raised an ancient rifle—Mills later swore it was a flintlock musket—shouted "Banzai!" and fired.

In the shears, Red Weaver cried out, "I'm hit! I'm hit!"

"Jesus H. Christ!" Mills shouted. "The dumb old bastard! Lookouts, clear the bridge! Weaver, can you make it?"

Bonsel, Weaver, and the third lookout climbed down out of the shears. Weaver was holding his left arm. There was blood on his sleeve.

Another shot rang out, and the bullet ricocheted through the shears.

"Get down!" Mills shouted. "Stupid bastard. Lookouts below!" Into the intercom, he shouted, "Weaver's wounded! Tell Doc. Away the boarding party."

"Wait a minute," Hunt said to Mills as they crouched beneath the fairwater. "Let me see if I can handle this without force."

"All right," said Mills. "Belay the boarding party. Have them stand by in the conning tower."

Hunt picked up the megaphone and shouted in Japanese, "We come in peace!"

"Peace?" a Japanese voice shouted back. "What joke is this?"

"We're sincere," Hunt said. "We are on an errand of mercy."

There was a long silence. "What kind of errand?"

"We have a Japanese child on board," Hunt said. "We wish to turn her—and some food—over to you."

Another silence.

"Where did you get a Japanese child?"

An awkward moment. Hunt took a deep breath, collected his thoughts, and said, "About a week ago in this area, we accidentally, and unfortunately, rammed a sampan in heavy fog. There was a—we were frightened—did not know what it was—we reacted like the seamen we've been trained to be. There was shooting. But we rescued the child."

"Was that the *Star of Miyake Jima?*"

"We do not know the name."

"You burned her?"

"Yes. We had to. She was impaled on our bow."

"You reacted like barbarians," the voice said. "Not seamen. You killed nine people. Poor, simple fishermen."

"We regret that," Hunt said. "We'd like to give you the child."

There was a long silence.

"We will take the child. Her mother was severely burned, but rescued. She's in the hospital in Tsubota Ko. She will be glad to hear that her child was returned in this miraculous manner."

Mills said to Hunt, "Watch it. Tell them no funny stuff."

"Do you have a dory?" Hunt asked the old man.

"Yes," he replied.

"All right," Hunt said. "We're going to pull off about a hundred meters. Send your dory alongside."

They moved *Shark* beyond flintlock musket range of the sampan, and they hove to. Shortly, they saw the dory pulling away from the vessel, the old man at the oars.

"Boarding party to the bridge," Mills said. "Bring up Lockwood-san."

Walker led his party to the bridge. Lockwood-san was cradled in his arms. The other five men carried Thompsons.

"Be goddamn careful," Mills said. "We've already had one man hit. The five of you deploy on deck. Cover Walker and the dory."

They went on the forward deck and deployed. Walker carried Lockwood-san to the starboard side, and Hunt yelled to the man, "We repeat, this is an errand of mercy. Our men are armed because you shot at us. No more banzai."

"No banzai," the man replied, pulling on the oars.

He came alongside skillfully, and Walker gave Lockwood-san a last cuddle and a kiss on her head and passed her into the man's arms.

"We want to give you food," Hunt called out, "for the child and her mother."

"All right," the old man said.

"Okay," said Mills. "Bring up the food."

Lyman, Webster, Martinez, and the two mess cooks came up carrying half a dozen burlap bags and heavy boxes. Mills said, "For Pete's sake, Freddie, what the hell are you giving them?"

"Potatoes, rice, beef, pork, butter, a gross of condensed milk tins, powdered milk and eggs, bacon, sausage, canned juice, and so on."

"Did you leave anything for us?" said Mills.

"Oh, yes, sir," Lyman said. "This is going to be a brief patrol. There's plenty left for us."

"Very well," said Mills. "Try not to swamp the dory."

They took the food on deck and passed it over to the old man. When the dory was all loaded, it was nearly awash. They watched as the old man rowed back to the sampan.

"Sayonara," Hunt called out.

"Sayonara," the old man replied.

"All hands below!" Mills shouted. "All ahead full."

*Shark* nosed ahead, suddenly enveloped in dense fog. This time the fog was welcome, for it would shield them from aircraft searchlights, and they could once again use the SJ radar. Hunt made a final fix on Mikura Jima, and *Shark* turned east, leaving behind Nampo Shoto and the heavily patrolled waters. Nothing lay between them and Majuro but open sea.

In the wardroom, Mills sipped a cup of coffee. He said to Martinez, "Find Willie Bonsel, and tell him I'm ready to resume our cribbage match."

# CHAPTER SIXTY-THREE

Pierpont pushed his way into the crew's mess which was jammed with off-watch sailors noisily talking and laughing. Tokyo Rose, turned loud, was playing "Chattanooga Choo-Choo." Pierpont made his way to a corner where Red Weaver, wearing no shirt and looking glum, was seated on a bench. Doc Jones was dressing his arm.

"How is it?" said Pierpont.

"Just a superficial flesh wound," said Jones, dabbing the arm with alcohol. "A scratch."

"Ouch!" said Weaver, pulling his arm away.

"For God's sake, Red," said Jones, "will you calm down? Stop trying to make a medical discharge out of this silly wound."

"You were sure right about one thing," Pierpont said to Weaver. "There *was* a bullet out there with your name on it. Some bullet! What a fraud!"

"It's no joke," said Weaver. "You've never been shot. That old fart could have killed me!"

"Quit your bitching," said Pierpont. "You'll get a Purple Heart for that."

Weaver beamed. "That's right. I never thought of that."

"What about Vogel?" said Jones. "Do you get a Purple Heart for spraining your ankle?"

"I don't know," said Pierpont. "I'll have to look that up."

"If Vogel gets a Purple Heart," said Weaver, "then Weir is entitled to one, too, isn't he? I mean, he broke a leg."

"That son of a bitch gets a swift kick in the ass," Jones said. "That's what he gets."

"Do I get light duty?" Weaver said as Jones put the final touches on the bandage.

"Are you kidding?" Pierpont sneered. "You've got to type up the patrol report, the transfers, the—"

"Aw, come on, Bob," Weaver said. "How often does a yeoman get shot, for Christ's sake?"

"Blow it out your ass," Pierpont said, playfully punching Weaver in the stomach. "Get to work."

Childress came into the mess carrying a chart with *Shark*'s track from Mikura Jima to Majuro Atoll neatly laid out with estimated rates of advance by days. He tacked it on the bulletin board, and Pierpont scrutinized it with a practiced eye. Not a bad job.

"You going to go for qualification this run?" said Pierpont.

"Yes," said Childress. "Mr. Hunt's going to take me through the boat tomorrow. Man, am I nervous!"

"Don't worry. You'll do okay. Don't forget that bypass valve in control for—"

"Shifting the two-hundred-pound air system to blow negative."

"Right," said Pierpont, much pleased with his protégé. "You handling the anchor pool?"

"Got it," said Childress, tapping his shirt pocket where he kept the roster.

"Good man," Pierpont said. He lowered his voice. "You qualify this patrol, I'm going to put you in for spot promotion to first class."

*"What?"* said Childress. He was dumb struck.

"You can handle it," said Pierpont. "You're a quick study, Childress. By the way, you can be sure the Old Man won't forget that you volunteered to rig that line. Topside; submerged. In Tokyo Bay. That's about the gutsiest thing I've ever seen."

Tony Walker came into the mess looking for Freddie Lyman. He found him in the galley, chopping meat. "Christ, Freddie," said Walker, "I said 190 bucks worth. How much more do I owe you?"

"Forget it," Lyman said. "We'll hide it." He poised his meat cleaver in midair. "I miss that little rascal, even if she did nearly get us zapped for good."

"I miss her, too," said Walker, "but I guess the Old Man was right. She's better off where she is."

"No matter what happens to the Japs, she won't starve," Lyman said, bringing the cleaver down. "Fishermen never starve. Even in the Depression, our fishermen ate well."

Pierpont pushed aft to the crew's sleeping quarters where he found Weir reading in his bunk, flashlight over his shoulder. He said, "How you doing?"

"Better."

"We'll be home soon," said Pierpont. "Get you to a sick bay."

"I'll have to leave the boat?"

"Sure. You're not much good to us with a broken leg."

"Can I get on another boat, later?"

Pierpont weighed this. "You know, they were going to disqualify you from submarines?"

"Me?" Weir said in astonishment. "Why?"

"Why? Don't you have the slightest clue of what you're like, you asshole? You're a smart ass. You don't do what you're told. You dream up weird diseases. You mouth off at the officers. Show no respect."

"I didn't realize that," Weir said sincerely.

"Well, for Christ's sake," said Pierpont. "You *are* a case."

"Can you help me?" Weir said with a note of desperation. "Put in a good word for me?"

"Can you change your goddamned attitude?"

"Yes, *sir!*" Weir said.

"Don't sir me," Pierpont said. "Sir the officers, for Christ's sake."

"Will you help me?" Weir repeated, pleading.

"Frankly, Weir, until you went up into that conning tower to fix the SJ, I wouldn't have recommended you as dogcatcher. I'll tell you what. You give me your goddamn word you'll change your attitude, I'll put in a good word for you."

"Yes, sir!"

"Oh shit, Weir. You're hopeless."

He went forward to the chiefs' quarters. Pops Wheeler said, "Did you get the word? Willie the Silent just beat the shit out of the Old Man. He won the fucking tournament."

"I'll be gone to hell," said Pierpont.

"I could hear it all the way in here," Wheeler said. "The Old Man cussing like a thirty-year man. You know how he hates to lose. Anything."

"What did Willie say?"

"Not a goddamn word. He just got up and walked out of the wardroom."

# CHAPTER SIXTY-FOUR

Admiral Lockwood and his chief of staff, Sunshine Murray, greeted Mills in the flag officers' dining room on *Holland*. Lockwood and Murray had flown from Pearl Harbor to Majuro overnight. The three men took seats at the table and gave their orders to the mess steward.

"I've read your report," Lockwood said to Mills, "and I want to extend my heartiest congratulations to you and all hands. It has to be the most outstanding patrol of the war. What a story it will make someday. When it can be told."

"Thank you, sir," Mills said.

"Admiral Nimitz asked me to extend you a personal well-done," Lockwood went on. "He asked to add an endorsement for your report, and I assure you it will be a stem-winder. You've probably provided the most important weapons intelligence of the war. They are already working on defenses, though I don't know what they might be. He was also grateful for the excellent poop on *Yamato* and *Musashi*. Not to mention the photos of Yokosuka. And our technical boys are grateful—as am I—for Bell's conjecture about the Japs being able to home on the SJ radar. They think he's right."

The steward served cold chef's salad and fresh milk.

"I suppose you've heard I got that ridiculous BuPers personnel rotation policy rescinded?" Lockwood went on.

"No, sir," Mills said, brightening.

"I should say modified," Lockwood corrected. "I will decide when a skipper's had enough. The enlisted men will be given a choice of staying on or leaving, with, of course, approval of the individual commanding officers."

They ate silently for a moment. Mills was literally sitting on the edge of his chair in anticipation. You don't hurry an admiral to his point.

"The squadron engineers tell me that *Shark* will need a yard overhaul," said Lockwood. "Pearl Harbor is jammed, so I'm ordering *Shark* to Mare Island for overhaul and modernization."

Mills beamed. At least three months in San Francisco! The crew would go wild when they heard the news.

"You're not going to like what I have to say next," said Lockwood.

Mills felt a chill inside. He took a sip of milk, his eyes on the admiral.

"I'm sending you to new construction."

"But admiral—"

"No 'but admirals' this time," Lockwood said sternly. "You've made nine consecutive war patrols. You need a good long blow on the beach. You'll be relieved here and fly back to the States."

"Yes, sir," said Mills, feeling as though he were caught in a whirlpool and being slowly sucked into the sea.

"Last but not least," Lockwood went on, dabbing his mouth with the linen napkin, "I'm putting you in for a Medal of Honor. I've cleared it with Nimitz, so it'll move right on up to CNO."

Mills was stupefied.

"Congratulations," said Sunshine Murray, extending a hand across the table. "Very much earned—and deserved."

"That will make you the single most decorated sub skipper in the U.S. Navy," Lockwood said. "It won't hurt you after the war. If you stay out of china shops, you could move up to flag rank.

Meanwhile, the War Bond Drive people will be after you. I know you hate to make speeches, but your representation in that public area wouldn't hurt the sub force."

"Yes, sir, admiral," said Mills, his mind whirling. He was giddy.

"Your Medal of Honor," Lockwood continued, "means that you—and the crew of *Shark*—are authorized a sizable number of lesser awards. One Navy Cross. Ten Silver Stars. Fifteen Bronze Crosses. I'd expect to have your recommendations before you shove off for the States."

"Yes, sir," said Mills. "The Navy Cross should go to Bill Hunt."

"Yes, of course," said Lockwood. "I agree completely."

Mills was wondering who most deserved the Silver Stars. Walker and Vogel for the shore party. Childress for rigging the line. Kilpatrick and Bonsel for going in the trim tank. But . . .

"Admiral," said Mills, "I know the usual policy is to award the Silver Stars to the officers. But, if it meets with your approval, sir, I'd like to give them to the enlisted men."

Lockwood looked up in surprise. "The recommendation is entirely up to you. Frankly, I like it. The enlisted men have gotten far too little recognition when it comes to gongs."

"Yes, sir," said Mills. "That's the way I see it. Ah, sir, I'd also like to spot promote my pharmacist's mate, Jones, to warrant."

"Certainly," Lockwood said. "Well deserved. Put the paper through."

"Who will be my relief, sir?" Mills asked.

"I've been talked into dropping down to the class of '37," Lockwood said. "We agree with your assessment. Bill Hunt is fully qualified for command. He will command *Shark*. And by the way, your former exec, Mike Reynolds, will also get a command." He smiled and added, "It would seem you run a pretty heads-up combat course out there, Mills."

Lockwood rolled his napkin and tucked it in the silver ring. He looked at Mills with a faint grin. "By the way, I heard you named that Jap baby Lockwood-san."

"Where could you have heard that, sir?" Mills said, his face turning crimson.

"I liked it, Mills," Lockwood said. "I was touched."

## ABOUT THE AUTHORS

CLAY and JOAN BLAIR have been a writing team for the last nine years. Their joint efforts have produced four previous novels: *The Board Room*, *The Archbishop*, *Pentagon Country* and *Scuba!*, as well as numerous works of non-fiction, including *The Strange Case of James Earl Ray*, *Survive!* (which was made into a major motion picture), *Silent Victory*, *Combat Patrol*, *The Search for J.F.K.* and *MacArthur*. The Blairs currently live in Florida.

# Coming Soon!

## The 2nd exciting book in
## THE SUBMARINERS
### series

---

## SWORDRAY MISSION

---

### BY CLAY & JOAN BLAIR

America's crack new submarine, *Swordray*, stationed in Manila Bay, is rushed into action as a result of the bombing of Pearl Harbor. As the Japanese forces begin to overrun the South Pacific, the *Swordray* must patrol the dangerous waters carrying out daring assignments to sink a carrier and to evacuate over sixteen million dollars worth of Philippine gold.

# BANTAM WAR BOOKS

These action-packed books recount the most important events of World War II. They take you into battle and present portraits of brave men and true stories of gallantry in action. All books have special maps, diagrams, and illustrations.

| | | | |
|---|---|---|---|
| ☐ | 12657 | **AS EAGLES SCREAMED** Burgett | $2.25 |
| ☐ | 12658 | **THE BIG SHOW** Clostermann | $2.25 |
| ☐ | 13014 | **BRAZEN CHARIOTS** Crisp | $2.25 |
| ☐ | 12666 | **THE COASTWATCHERS** Feldt | $2.25 |
| ☐ | *12664 | **COCKLESHELL HEROES** Lucas-Phillips | $2.25 |
| ☐ | 12916 | **COMPANY COMMANDER** MacDonald | $2.25 |
| ☐ | 12578 | **THE DIVINE WIND** Pineau & Inoguchi | $2.25 |
| ☐ | *12669 | **ENEMY COAST AHEAD** Gibson | $2.25 |
| ☐ | *12667 | **ESCORT COMMANDER** Robertson | $2.25 |
| ☐ | 12927 | **THE FIRST AND THE LAST** Galland | $2.25 |
| ☐ | *11642 | **FLY FOR YOUR LIFE** Forrester | $1.95 |
| ☐ | 12665 | **HELMET FOR MY PILLOW** Leckie | $2.25 |
| ☐ | 12663 | **HORRIDO!** Toliver & Constable | $2.25 |
| ☐ | 12670 | **THE HUNDRED DAYS OF LT. MACHORTON** Machorton | $2.25 |
| ☐ | *12668 | **I FLEW FOR THE FUHRER** Knoke | $2.25 |
| ☐ | 12290 | **IRON COFFINS** Werner | $2.25 |
| ☐ | 12671 | **QUEEN OF THE FLAT-TOPS** Johnston | $2.25 |
| ☐ | *11822 | **REACH FOR THE SKY** Brickhill | $1.95 |
| ☐ | 12662 | **THE ROAD PAST MANDALAY** Masters | $2.25 |
| ☐ | 12523 | **SAMURAI** Sakai with Caidin & Saito | $2.25 |
| ☐ | 12659 | **U-BOAT KILLER** Macintyre | $2.25 |
| ☐ | 12660 | **V-2** Dornberger | $2.25 |
| ☐ | *12661 | **THE WHITE RABBIT** Marshall | $2.25 |
| ☐ | *12150 | **WE DIE ALONE** Howarth | $1.95 |

**\*Cannot be sold to Canadian Residents.**

Buy them at your local bookstore or use this handy coupon:

Bantam Books, Inc., Dept. WW2, 414 East Golf Road, Des Plaines, Ill. 60016

Please send me the books I have checked above. I am enclosing $_____ (please add 75¢ to cover postage and handling). Send check or money order —no cash or C.O.D.'s please.

Mr/Mrs/Miss _____

Address _____

City _____ State/Zip _____

WW2—10/79

Please allow four weeks for delivery. This offer expires 4/80.

# Bantam Book Catalog

Here's your up-to-the-minute listing of over 1,400 titles by your favorite authors.

This illustrated, large format catalog gives a description of each title. For your convenience, it is divided into categories in fiction and non-fiction—gothics, science fiction, westerns, mysteries, cookbooks, mysticism and occult, biographies, history, family living, health, psychology, art.

So don't delay—take advantage of this special opportunity to increase your reading pleasure.

Just send us your name and address and 50¢ (to help defray postage and handling costs).

**BANTAM BOOKS, INC.**
Dept. FC, 414 East Golf Road, Des Plaines, Ill. 60016

Mr./Mrs./Miss_____
(please print)

Address_____

City_____State_____Zip_____

Do you know someone who enjoys books? Just give us their names and addresses and we'll send them a catalog too!

Mr./Mrs./Miss_____

Address_____

City_____State_____Zip_____

Mr./Mrs./Miss_____

Address_____

City_____State_____Zip_____

FC—9/78